Donald Duk

Donald Duk

A NOVEL BY FRANK CHIN

COFFEE HOUSE PRESS ⚱ MINNEAPOLIS

This new edition of *Donald Duk* has been rechecked by the publisher and author.

Coffee House Press is a nonprofit publishing house that presents literature of our time to a national audience. Our publishing program is made possible through sales of books and by grants from foundations, corporate giving programs, and state and federal arts agencies. Annual support has been provided by the Cowels Media/Star Tribune, Dayton Hudson Foundation, General Mills Foundation, Honeywell Foundation, Jerome Foundation, Lannan Foundation, McKnight Foundation, St. Paul Companies, and the Minnesota State Arts Board. Major funding has been received for special projects from the Andrew W. Mellon Foundation.

Coffee House Press books are available to bookstores through our primary distributor, Consortium Book Sales and Distribution, 1045 Westgate Drive, St. Paul, MN 55114-1065. Our books are also available through all major library distributors and jobbers, and through most small press distributors. For personal orders, catalogs, or other information, write to:

COFFEE HOUSE PRESS
27 No. Fourth Street, Suite 400, Minneapolis, MN 55401

Chin, Frank, 1940–
   Donald Duk : a novel / by Frank Chin
   p.   cm.
Summary: On the eve of the Chinese New Year in San Francisco's Chinatown, twelve-year-old Donald Duk attempts to deal with his comical name and his feelings for his cultural heritage.
ISBN 0-918273-83-8

[1. Chinese Americans – Fiction. 2. Chinatown (San Francisco, Calif.) – Fiction]
I. Title.
PZ7.C4423DO 1991
[Fic]—DC 20   090-29994
                                          CIP
                                          AC
Second edition
10   9   8   7   6   5   4   3   2   1

for John Fisher

The night we ran, boy,
Nobody's faster
Sleeper's inside never woke
We were afraid of guns

1

WHO WOULD BELIEVE anyone named Donald Duk dances like Fred Astaire? Donald Duk does not like his name. Donald Duk never liked his name. He hates his name. He is not a duck. He is not a cartoon character. He does not go home to sleep in Disneyland every night. The kids that laugh at him are very smart. Everyone at his private school is smart. Donald Duk is smart. He is a gifted one, they say.

No one in school knows he takes tap dance lessons from a man who calls himself "The Chinese Fred Astaire." Mom talks Dad into paying for the lessons and tap shoes.

Fred Astaire. Everybody everywhere likes Fred Astaire in the old black-and-white movies. Late at night on TV, even Dad smiles when Fred Astaire dances. Mom hums along. Donald Duk wants to live the late-night life in old black-and-white movies and talk with his feet like Fred Astaire, and smile Fred Astaire's sweet lemonade smile.

The music teacher and English teacher in school go dreamy-eyed when they talk about seeing Fred Astaire and Ginger Rogers on the late-night TV. "Remember when he danced with Barbara Stanwyck? What was the name of that movie. . . ?"

"Barbara Stanwyck?"

"Did you see the one where he dances with Rita Hayworth?"

"Oooh, Rita Hayworth!"

Donald Duk enjoys the books he reads in school. The math is a curious game. He is not the only Chinese in the private school. But he is the only Donald Duk. He avoids the other Chinese here. And the Chinese seem to avoid him. This school is a place where the Chinese are comfortable hating Chinese. "Only the Chinese are stupid enough to give a kid a stupid name like Donald Duk," Donald Duk says to himself. "And if the Chinese were that smart, why didn't they invent tap dancing?"

Donald Duk's father's name is King. King Duk. Donald hates his father's name. He hates being introduced with his father. "This is King Duk, and his son Donald Duk." Mom's name is Daisy. "That's Daisy Duk, and her son Donald." Venus Duk and Penny Duk are Donald's sisters. The girls are twins and a couple of years older than Donald.

His own name is driving him crazy! Looking Chinese is driving him crazy! All his teachers are making a big deal about Chinese stuff in their classes because of Chinese New Year coming on soon. The teacher of California History is so happy to be reading about the Chinese. "The man I studied history under at Berkeley authored this book. He was a spellbinding lecturer," the teacher throbs. Then he reads, "'The Chinese in America were made passive and nonassertive by centuries of Confucian thought and Zen mysticism. They were totally unprepared for the violently individualistic and democratic Americans. From their first step on American soil to the middle of the twentieth century, the timid, introverted Chinese have been helpless against the relentless victimization by aggressive, highly competitive Americans.'

"'One of the Confucian concepts that lends the Chinese vulnerable to the assertive ways of the West is *the mandate of heaven*. As the European kings of old ruled by divine right, so the emperors of China ruled by the mandate of heaven.'" The teacher takes a breath and looks over his spellbound class. Donald wants to barf pink and green stuff all over the teacher's teacher's book.

"What's he saying?" Donald Duk's pal Arnold Azalea asks in a whisper.

"Same thing as everybody—Chinese are artsy, cutesy and chickendick," Donald whispers back.

Oh, no! Here comes Chinese New Year again! It is Donald Duk's worst time of year. Here come the stupid questions about the funny things Chinese believe in. The funny things Chinese do. The funny things Chinese eat. And, "Where can I buy some Chinese firecrackers?"

And in Chinatown it's *Goong hay fot choy* everywhere. And some gang kids do sell firecrackers. And some gang kids rob other kids looking for firecrackers. He doesn't like the gang kids. He doesn't like speaking their Chinese. He doesn't have to—this is America. He doesn't like Chinatown. But he lives here.

The gang kids know him. They call him by name. One day the Frog Twins wobble onto the scene with their load of full shopping bags. There is Donald Duk. And there are five gang boys and two girlfriends chewing gum, swearing and smirking. The gang kids wear black tanker jackets, white tee shirts and baggy black denim jeans. It is the alley in front of the Chinese Historical Society Museum. There are fish markets on each side of the Chinatown end of the alley. Lawrence Ferlinghetti's famous City Lights Bookstore is at the end that opens on Columbus Street. Suddenly there are the Frog Twins in their heavy black overcoats. They seem to be wearing all the clothes they own under their coats. Their coats bulge. Under their skirts they wear several pairs of trousers and slacks. They wear one knit cap over the other. They wear scarves tied over their heads and shawls over their shoulders.

That night, after he is asleep, Dad comes home from the restaurant and wakes him up. "You walk like a sad softie," Dad says. "You look like you want everyone to beat you up."

"I do not!" Donald Duk says.

"You look at yourself in the mirror," Dad says, and Donald Duk looks at himself in his full-length dressing mirror. "Look at those slouching shoulders, that pouty face. Look at those hands holding onto each other. You look scared!" Dad's voice booms and Donald hears everyone's feet hit the floor. Mom and the twins are out in the hall looking into his open door.

"I am scared!" Donald Duk says.

"I don't care if you are scared," Dad says. His eyes sizzle into Donald Duk's frightened pie-eyed stare. "Be as scared as you want to be, but don't look scared. Especially when you walk through Chinatown."

"How do I look like I'm not scared if I *am* scared?" Donald Duk asks.

"You walk with your back straight. You keep your hands out of your pockets. Don't hunch your shoulders. Think of them as being down. Keep your head up. Look like you know where you're going. Walk like you know where you're going. And you say, 'Don't mess with me, horsepuckie! Don't mess with me!' But you don't say it with your mouth. You say it with your eyes. You say it with your hands where everybody can see them. Anybody get two steps in front of you, you zap them with your eyes, and they had better nod at you or look away. When they nod, you nod. When you walk like nobody better mess with you, nobody will mess with you. When you walk around like you're walking now, all rolled up in a little ball and hiding out from everything, they'll get you for sure."

Donald does not like his dad waking him up like that and yelling at him. But what the old man says works. Outside among the cold San Francisco shadows and the early morning shoppers, Donald Duk hears his father's voice and straightens his back, takes his hands out of his pockets, says "Don't mess with me!" with his eyes and every move of his body. And, yes, he's talking with his body the way Fred Astaire talks, and shoots every gang kid who walks toward him in the eye with a look that says, "Don't mess with me." And no one messes with him. Dad never talks about it again.

Later, gang kids laugh at his name and try to pick fights with him during the afternoon rush hour, Dad's busy time in the kitchen. Donald is smarter than these lowbrow beady-eyed goons. He has to beat them without fighting them because he doesn't know how to fight. Donald Duk gets the twins to talk about it with Dad while they are all at the dining room table working on their model airplanes.

Dad laughs. "So he has a choice. He does not like people laughing at his name. He does not want the gangsters laughing at his name to beat him up. He mostly does not want to look like a sissy in front of them, so what can he do?"

"He can pay them to leave him alone," Venus says.

"He can not! That is so chicken it's disgusting!" Penelope says.

"So, our little brother is doomed."

"He can agree with them and laugh at his name," Dad says. "He can tell them lots of Donald Duk jokes. Maybe he can learn to talk that quack-quack Donald Duck talk."

"Whaaat?" the twins ask in one voice.

"If he keeps them laughing," Dad says, "even if he can just keep them listening, they are not beating him up, right? And they are not calling him a sissy. He does not want to fight? He does not have to fight. He has to use his smarts, okay? If he's smart enough, he makes up some Donald Duck jokes to surprise them and make them laugh. They laugh three times, he can walk away. Leave them there laughing, thinking Donald Duk is one terrific fella."

"So says King Duk," Venus Duk flips. The twins often talk as if everything they hear everybody say and see everybody do is dialog in a memoir they're writing or action in a play they're directing. This makes Mom feel like she's on stage and drives Donald Duk crazy.

"Is that Chinese psychology, dear?" Daisy Duk asks.

"Daisy Duk inquires," says Penelope Duk.

"And little Donnie Duk says, *Oh, Mom!* and sighs."

"I do not!" Donald Duk yelps at the twins.

"Well, then, say it," Penelope Duk says. "It's a good line. So *you* you, you know."

"Thank you," Venus says.

"Oh goshes, you all, your sympathy is so . . . so . . . so literary. So dramatic," Donald Duk says. "It is truly depressing."

"I thought it was narrative," Venus says.

"Listen up for some Chinese psychology, girls and boys," Daisy Duk says.

"No, that's not psychology, that's Bugs Bunny," Dad says.

"You don't mean Bugs Bunny, dear. You always make that mistake."

"Br'er Rabbit!" Dad says.

"What does that mean?" Donald Duk asks the twins. They shrug their shoulders. Nobody knows what Br'er Rabbit has to do with Dad's way of avoiding a fight and not being a fool, but it works.

One bright and sunny afternoon, a gang boy stops Donald and talks to him in the quacking voice of Walt Disney's Donald Duck. The voice breaks Donald Duk's mind for a flash, and he is afraid to turn on his own Donald Duck voice. He tries telling a joke about Donald Duck not wearing trousers or shoes, when the gangster—in black jeans, black tee shirt, black jacket, black shades—says in a perfect Donald Duck voice, "Let's take the pants off Donald Duk!"

"Oh oh! I stepped in it now!" Donald Duk says in his Donald Duck voice and stuns the gangster and his two gangster friends and their three girlfriends. Everything is seen and understood very fast. Without missing a beat, his own perfect Donald Duck voice cries for help in perfect Cantonese *Gow meng ahhhh!* and they all laugh. Old women pulling little wire shopping carts full of fresh vegetables stop and stare at him. Passing children recognize the voice and say Donald Duck talks Chinese.

"Don't let these monsters take off my pants. I may be Donald Duk, but I am as human as you," he says in Chinese, in his Donald Duck voice, "I know how to use chopsticks. I use flush toilets. Why shouldn't I wear pants on Grant Street in Chinatown?" They all laugh more than three times. Their laughter roars three times on the corner of Grant and Jackson, and Donald Duk walks away, leaving them laughing, just the way Dad says he can. He feels great. Just great!

Donald Duk does not want to laugh about his name forever. There has to be an end to this. There is an end to all kidstuff for a kid. An end to diapers. An end to nursery rhymes and fairy tales. There has to be an end to laughing about his name to get out of a fight. Chinese New Year. Everyone will be laughing. He is twelve years old. Twelve years old is special to the Chinese. There are twelve years in the Asian lunar zodiac. For each year there is an animal. This year Donald will complete his first twelve-year cycle of his life. To celebrate, Donald Duk's father's old opera mentor, Uncle Donald Duk, is coming to San Francisco to perform a Cantonese opera. Donald Duk does not want Chinese New Year. He does not want his Uncle Donald Duk to tell him again how Daddy was a terrible man to name his little boy Donald Duk, because all the *bokgwai,* the white monsters, will think he is named after that barebutt cartoon duck in the top half of a sailor suit and no shoes.

2

EVERYONE IN SCHOOL knows that Donald Duk's uncle, Donald Duk, the Cantonese opera entrepreneur and star, is coming to the school. The whole school is set to assemble in the auditorium, where Uncle Donald will appear in Cantonese opera costume and makeup and do a bit of opera that will make no kind of sense to the school and embarrass Donald Duk. No, Donald does not want his uncle to come. It will be awful. Everything Chinese in his life seems to be awful. His father is awful.

Daddy has an awful Chinatown accent. Daddy is not rich. He is not poor, either. He owns a successful Chinatown restaurant. He is the best cook there. In Chinatown they say he is one of the best seven.

It is a Chinese kitchen in a Chinese restaurant. All deep iron woks, gas griddles and grills in a line against one wall. Dad never complains or stops smiling when Donald Duk asks for what he thinks is pure American food. Steaks. Chops. One night Arnold Azalea stays for dinner in the kitchen. Donald Duk asks Dad for a French fish stew he's read about in the newspaper. He asks for bouillabaisse. And his father makes bouillabaisse. He chops the

onions with his Chinese cleaver. He talks about the difference between pure French cooking and the French-with-the-Chinese-
twist cooking he does. Dad says he can make Spanish paella or
Italian cioppino too, or anything Donald wants to eat. During the
last war, Dad says, he is on the security staff of the U.S. Army chief
of staff, a four-star general who travels the world and answers only
to the commander in chief.

"I learned to cook in the kitchens of the most powerful men in
the world, keeping my eye on the chefs," Dad says often. A ham-
burger, an omelet, a chicken-fried steak starts Dad telling the story
of how he passed the war in the kitchens of presidents, prime min-
isters, premiers, lords and generalissimos. "But you know, the best
kitchen in the world was Chiang Kai-shek's. His chefs were all
Cantonese.

"And they could cook everything—Italian, Greek, French,
Spanish, Brazilian—they did it all. I asked them, Why? And they
said, Chiang never entertains other Chinese, only Europeans, who
can stand to eat only one Chinese banquet a month. And Chiang
wants all his foreign visitors to feel at home, in their noses, palates
and taste buds. That's what they tell me. And I learn a lot from
them. I learn from all of them."

Donald Duk's best friend, Arnold Azalea, and his mother and
father eat in Donald Duk's father's Chinatown restaurant now
and then. Sometimes they bring friends. The adults do not mind
being left alone at the table and are happy to let Arnold join Donald in the kitchen. The boys sit on Chinese stools at two places set
on the kitchen chopping block and challenge the extent of Dad's
knowledge of food and cooking. Whatever the boys read about
and ask for, Dad cooks without a book. Whatever it is, he cooks it.
It's become a game that sends the boys to the library reading books
about food.

One night out with his parents and their friends, Arnold Azalea
asks if he can spend the night at Donald Duk's, in Chinatown.
Donald Duk does not ask Arnold to stay over. He never thought

of asking anyone over to his house. His house is too Chinese. Arnold's father excuses himself from the table and goes back into the kitchen to talk with Donald's dad.

"King," Arnold's dad says, "my boy has just invited himself to spend the night at your house with Donald."

Donald's dad looks over his shoulder between the stainless steel shelves of the steam table to see Arnold's dad. He grins and speaks with both of his hands busy flashing and clanging a long-handled spoon and spatula against the sides of a round-bottomed wok. He scoops and spoons diced chicken in a light sauce out of the wok onto a serving dish, in three moves. "Sure! We're happy to have him over. He can stay in Donald's room."

"And we'd be happy to have Donald spend a night or a weekend with Arnold. The boys are such close friends."

"Sure. No problem," Donald Duk's father says.

There are two old Chinatown sisters. Twins. Scrunched-up old Chinatown women who have exactly the same eyes. Frog eyes. Their eyes seem to bulge out of their heads. They wait outside Dad's restaurant when the garbage is put out. Now and then, when Dad knows they are out in the alley, he gives them a fresh catfish to take home. Or a piece of Chinese sidemeat people like to steam in a pot with taro root and potato. Dad is nice to them because they are twins, like Donald Duk's older sisters. Donald Duk calls the old twins "the Frog Twins." He thinks they look like frogs. He says they look like they eat flies.

On his time off from the restaurant, Dad builds model airplanes. He calls them "stick and paper" models of airplanes that flew in World War I and World War II. The next day Arnold cannot take his eyes off of all the large model airplanes hanging from the ceilings of the living room and dining room. Dad tells him he is building 108 little airplanes. "One for each of the 108 outlaw heroes of a famous Chinese book I read when I was a kid."

"What are you going to do with them?"

"I'm going to fly them all off of Angel Island on the fifteenth day of the Chinese New Year," Dad says.

"I wish I could see that," Arnold says. Donald cannot believe it. Arnold likes Chinese food. He asks about the stories in the book about the 108 outlaw heroes. And, oh no! before Donald knows it, Arnold is sleeping over the whole two weeks before the parade, and Dad enrolls them both in his friend's White Crane Kung Fu Club, so Donald and Arnold can both run inside the long dragon lantern during the Chinese New Year parade.

"Then after the parade we'll go to Angel Island and fly the model airplanes," Arnold says. He sounds like he can't wait. He sounds like he wants to run inside the stupid dragon, wants to fly the stupid model airplanes Dad and the twins built.

"No, after the opera," says Dad.

"The opera?"

"Cantonese opera. My old opera *sifu,* the original Donald Duk, is bringing his company to town to perform a special Cantonese opera for the New Year, the same night of the parade. Big night. The night of lights and lovers. After the opera, you and your folks, we will all go with the opera people for a little banquet. You boys will be staying up very late. Yes, well past midnight into the early morning before the sun rises. Then we will board my chartered boat and cross the water to Angel Island. I'm going to set them all afire and launch them. And all the planes will fly. And all the planes will burn."

Donald is as shocked as his friend Arnold. Dad never said he planned to burn all the little airplanes. Dad and the twins worked years to build these planes. Now Dad says he wants to burn them all up the first time they fly? "Why?" Donald asks.

"The mandate of heaven. *Tien ming* "

"What's that?" Donald asks and remembers Mr. Meanwright's saying the Chinese mandate of heaven is why Chinese are cutesy chickendicks.

"The Chinese say, Kingdoms rise and fall. Nations come and go," Dad says.

"What does that mean?"

"Nothing is good forever. What goes up will come down. Times change. Do not get hang up on your own bullsquish. Do not fall in love with your good looks. Don't marry your stool pigeon."

"What's that mean?" Donald asks.

"You and your pal Arnold are going to learn what that means before the night of the parade, or you're not running inside the dragon."

"I don't want to run inside the dragon. Arnold wants to run inside the dragon, not me!" Donald Duk says.

"You're his host. He is your guest. He runs, you run. If I do your friend a favor, I am doing you a favor. Understand that right now or I'll stop doing you favors and Arnold can go home."

Donald cools it.

"What does *stool pigeon* mean, Mr. Duk?" Arnold asks.

"It means fink, tattletale, stool pigeon kind of people."

Donald Duk thinks he understands why Arnold is being so geewhiz gah-gah mouth about Dad's toy planes. Donald hates to see his friend pretend to be so nice to Chinese with stupid names like Duk. Donald Duk has as little to do with any of them as he can. Donald does not care what King, Daisy, Penny or Venus Duk do. If they want to build little airplanes on the dining room table night and day, Donald does not care. But he is a little surprised to hear Dad is going to burn them all.

Day after day, night after night, he passes the dining and front rooms on the way into and out of the apartment. He glances in at them going to or from the front room, where he watches TV. All the planes. All covered with colored tissue paper and painted with Chinese watercolors. Each plane has a little motor. Dad does not paint the models to look like the real planes of World War I and World War II. Instead, Dad paints faces on the noses, hands on the wings, and spears and bows and arrows and old-time Chinese weapons in the hands. And still the planes look kind of real, ready to fly.

If they are all going to burn anyway, why can't Donald Duk fly one and burn it himself? Donald Duk wonders about that every night before he falls asleep. Every time he walks past the rooms and looks over the planes, he is looking for the one plane Dad will not get all mad over when Donald burns it by himself.

He chooses a little stubby one. It is a P-26A. It looks like a little honeybee. The plane's wings are the same shape as a bee's wings. It also looks like a little sports car. A hand holding a short-handled battle-axe is painted on each wingtip. Donald goes to the library and looks up the P-26A, and reads about it, and finds pictures of it. The real P-26A was a warplane that never flew in a war, except in China, where it was shot out of the sky before Pearl Harbor. It was called the "Peashooter." The most famous of these planes had blue bodies and yellow wings. The rudder and horizontal stabilizer at the tail were yellow.

The colors of Dad's model P-26A are nothing like the real thing.

One night Donald Duk puts on his new sneakers in the dark and does not turn on the light. Arnold is asleep in the upper bunk. He is staying over every night of the Chinese New Year celebration . . . Tomorrow is the first day. He opens the door to his room and there is the dark of the empty hallway. He steps into the hall and looks through the dark to the front of the apartment. He is dressed in clean clothes. He even has a jacket on to keep out the cold he knows is upstairs on the roof.

3

DONALD DUK'S FLASHLIGHT has a bright hard beam. It casts shadows on the walls and ceiling. It shines through the tissue-paper wings and spills the shadows of ribs and spars on the ceiling. The shadows of wings and tails, wheels and struts, all move when the light moves. The flashlight beam hits the model plane on the bottom like the real searchlights of World War I, World War II and movie premieres. The P-26A was made between the wars. Americans never flew the Peashooter in war. Donald finds it. His heart beats a fast thump of slamming doors and crashing drawers in his ears. Donald Duk's heart beats so fast he's scared. He stops to listen. He hears a thousand hearts bouncing like handballs off the walls of his chest. He stops to hear if anybody else hears it. Can he hear sounds outside of his heart? He has not even touched the P-26A, and his heart is running like a thousand thieves. Donald Duk smells his sweat. He is hot.

He does not have time to take off his jacket if he's going to take the plane and go. The longer he stays, the more he does, the more likely he'll make a noise. He takes his flashlight and stands it on its end to shine straight up under the plane. He stands up on a chair and sees light around the edges of the p-26a. One hand gets a soft firm hold on the model by the belly. Don't squeeze too hard, or it will break. One hand uses scissors to cut the threads that hold the plane dangling from the ceiling. Quietly. Quietly. He smells of fresh sweat and is used to his fast heart going too loud. He picks up his flashlight and is out of the room.

Everyone loves looking down Chinatown main streets from the top of a Chinatown roof. People who live in Chinatown especially like the view from the roof. Not the roof of a high rise. Not the roof of the Holiday Inn. The right roof is the roof of a three-story building on Grant Street, like the roof of Donald Duk's building. He stands just above the streetlights. The crowds of people filling the sidewalk and spaces between cars jammed in the street are gone for the night.

Every day till Chinese New Year the crowds will get larger down there. At night they all seem to be bobbing at the bottom of a huge long pool of ice water. All their brightness, all their noise, all the rumble of their feet and the thumping of the automobile engines bounce up the faces of the three-story buildings on both sides of the street. Chinatown life lies against Donald Duk's cheek like a purring cat. He feels the purring in his teeth. He feels the purring in his toes. The giggling and mumbling, snickering cars plod slowly one way only down Grant toward Broadway, and the milling crowd flows all the time like algae in a marsh through Chinatown steadily as a river. Sometimes late at night the river slows down, way down and someone speeds a car from one end of Chinatown to the other. Someone screams. Someone plays music in the streets after the cars are gone. It is that late now. No cars. No crowds. The stores and shops and restaurants are almost all closed. Their lights are off. The face of their building is out of sight in the dark of the big night. Two-thirty in the morning, his digital wristwatch reads out. This is as dark as Chinatown gets. The only lights on now are the lights that never go out before dawn.

Some old man in the shadows of the bank on the corner sits on his heels and plays a double-stringed fiddle. It sounds like a singing

busy signal on the phone. It is much louder than a phone. Tonight
he hears a voice in the whining suffering sounds the old man plays.
No cars. No people. Only artificial light and music from the shadows.

Donald Duk starts the little p-26a's little glo-plug engine. It
sounds like fifty diving mosquitoes. He lights the fuse Dad built
into the plane, aims it up Grant Street toward California and lets
it fly out of his hand. The plane swoops down and away from
Donald Duk. He looks down on top of the plane. The hairy
brown hands on the wingtips make the plane look like a diving
man. The buzz of the little engine echoes up and down Grant. It
sounds like a honeybee. Down on Grant Street, the Frog Twins
wobble along with their shopping bags, side by side. Their thick
lenses flash. Twin knitted caps bag the tops of their heads. They
have come out to pick through the garbage set out by the restaurants after closing. The Frog Twins hear the sound of a giant honeybee and look up to see the glow of the streetlights catch in the
little plane's tissue-paper skin. The skin is full of twilight. They see
the face painted on the front around the little motor and the hands
and battle-axes on the wings. They gasp and give a little squeak in
their throats as they catch their breath.

The flight over the empty street is ghostly. The slowly slowly
flying body, painted-on nose and wings seem alive. The lenses of
the Frog Twin's glasses flash in Donald Duk's eyes, and he sees
them see him. Then, oh no! Fire flares up all over the plane. For an
instant, all the little wooden things Dad put together glow like
bones in the center of the flames. The glowing plane is feathered in
flames, and everything that will burn is all burnt up. The fire goes
out and disappears in midair over Chinatown about two blocks
further up the street. Then ashes and the humming engine and
twirling propeller drop to the ground.

The Frog Twins stare at the spot in the air with their mouths
open. Donald Duk can't feel himself breathing, the wobble and
whack of his heart are so loud, he can't hear, he can't walk and be

sure when his feet will touch the tin-clad roof that crunches under every step. Something plops his mouth shut. He can't breathe. A big hand is squeezing his face. A big hand holds him by the back of the neck. He looks into eyes like Dad's eyes. "Are you looking for me?" a voice asks in a Midwestern accent.

The hand lifts off Donald Duk's mouth. "No," Donald Duk says.

"What are you doing up here, kid?"

"I . . ." Donald Duk says, then suddenly in his Donald Duck voice of squishing quacks, "You must have seen, I came up just to fly my plane and, you saw it blow. You know, it blew up. It blew up!"

"Why're you talking like that? You think I'm funny?"

"I don't know. I . . . No. You're not funny."

"Do you believe me when I tell you I can break your nose just by doing this?" the Midwestern accent belongs to a thick, bulky Chinaman who flicks his index finger off his thumb into Donald Duk's chest. The nail side of the fingertip whips into Donald Duk and hurts. Donald Duk bends over the instant of pain. The spot hums now. There will be a mark. A bruise. "Yes," Donald Duk says. "I believe you."

"You live in the apartment right under the roof?"

"Yes," Donald Duk says. "Are you going to rob our place?"

"No, kid! That's against the law. I believe in the law. I fought for democracy. Forget robbery. Forget it. What's your name?"

"Are you Chinese?"

"No! I'm American. One hundred percent Iowa farmboy, United States Marine Corps, American. I fought the Chinese though. You think we were fighting the North Vietnamese regulars? I fought them. But they don't tell ya when you're going to fight Chinese. You don't want to fight the Chinese. I fought the Chinese. They'll hurt ya. They're bigger than the Vietnamese. Big feet. They're meaner. Real soldiers. Even dead they'll get ya. I asked you your name, right?"

"Who are you?" Donald Duk asks. "What do you want?"

"I'm the Cong, boy. The American Cong. Not the Viet Cong. American born, American trained, American Cong. And I don't want nothing but to hear your name. What is your name?"

"Donald Duk," Donald Duk says.

"You American?"

"Yeah."

"Okay, Donald Duk."

"You were in the Vietnam War?"

"I loved 'Nam. I had a good time there. I loved it. Really opened my eyes. Oooh." He breaks into wracking coughs and beats on his chest over his heart with his right fist, and eases himself down onto the roof to lie on his back.

"What's wrong?"

"Nothing! Stay where you are." He coughs some more and catches his breath. "I'm orange. You're Donald Duk. I'm orange."

"You're orange?"

"The big Orange out of the sky, Donald Duk. You're too young to remember. Do you know how strange, how weird that sounds, man? I'm talking to Donald Duck! I've seen all your movies, Donald!" the American Cong says. "The Vietnamese are wonderful people. They know how to live with nature."

"Nature?" Donald Duk scans the roof and sees many ways of climbing onto the roof, by the fire escape, from the roof of the next building . . .

"All they want is to farm, Donald Duk. That's all. The Montagnards. The Montagnards. That means 'Mountain People' in French. The hill tribes, wonderful people. They grow corn! Just like in Iowa. Corn! Here I am, no dog tags, no jewelry. No wallets. No labels. No patches. No insignia. Climb and hide for days to get to the Montagnards. And I crawl into a cornfield on the side of a motherin' mountain! A cornfield! Corn! I'm home again. They were fighting the Chinese. You don't want to fight the Chinese. They don't stop till they get you. And you don't want the Chinese to get you. They'll hurt ya. They'll hurt ya. No, you don't want the Chinese to get ya." He stops and clenches his teeth, tenses his body then suddenly lets go and crumples, falls over onto his left side like a collapsing hot air balloon.

"You need a doctor or something?"

"Forget it. They'll just tell me I'm orange. Big deal."

"What's orange?"

"It's like a big hand inside my chest's got my heart and squeezes. It hurts. And the heart beats fast then slow and skips. And that hurts. But 'Nam was good for me. I loved it. 'Nam wasn't good for everybody. Some boys started sucking their thumbs again. And some started crying *Momma momma momma, I love you!* and fall down sobbing, the first shot they hear! And when they get shot. *Oh, momma momma momma! I don't want to die!* Ha ha. It's funny, Donald Duk. Orange is not what you'd want to can as frozen juice. How'd you like to know that right here in the city parks, in the national parks and forests outside of town, there are bands of American Cong? Trained experienced guerrillas living like Robin Hood and his Merry Hairy Men, right now? You feel like camping in Yosemite with Huey, Dewey and Louie knowing your every move is being tracked, Donald Duk?"

"Is that where you live? Out in the forest?"

"I look too much like Charlie to them. Too many come back crazy to dink-a-dink when they come back from South Africa. Crazies who're still fighting the war they lost, man." He takes deeper breaths slowly into his mouth and stares at the few stars visible in the foamy dishwater dark overhead. "So, I'm here getting lost where everybody looks like Charlie and no one expects to find Americans."

"I'm an American."

"What do you know about America? I fought for America. I fought for freedom! I'm not asking anybody for anything. Did I ask you for anything? I'm not hurting anybody. Did I hurt you?"

"No," Donald Duk says and still feels where the American

Cong's fingertip whacked his chest. Donald Duk steps back from American Cong, who seems to be breathing a little easier. "Have you eaten dinner yet?"

American Cong breathes and relaxes. Donald Duk takes a ten-dollar bill out of his wallet.

"I don't want your money! I don't want anything from you. Just leave me alone!"

Donald Duk sees American Cong has no strength for fast moves right now, so he stuffs the ten-dollar bill into a pocket on the sleeve of Cong's camouflage field jacket and jumps back. "You're on my roof, that makes you my guest. You can't refuse," Donald Duk says and darts into the building and locks the door to the roof from inside. American Cong is very strong, very scary when he's not orange, and very sad in Donald Duk's instant replay downstairs to the carpeted hallway to his apartment.

Donald Duk's heart thumps hard and fast. So hard he feels every thump inside his chest. It beats so hard it is hard to breathe. He is as quiet as he can be, climbing down the stairs off the roof into the building again and slipping into his dark apartment.

No one is up in the front room watching the TV. No one is up using the bathroom. No lights on. Nothing has changed since he left with the little P-26A. Donald Duk steps one silent step after the other into his apartment and past the doors to the front room and the dining room. He shines his flashlight in to see if the room looks that much different with one little plane gone. His light hits a face! "Where's my Lee Kuey?"

"Uncle Donald!"

"What did you do with my Black Tornado?"

"What?" Donald Duk doesn't ask if he means the American Cong on the roof. Already Donald Duk is keeping the American Cong secret.

"My airplane! I saw you climb on a chair and take it down."

"I didn't see you."

"I didn't want you to."

"You won't tell Dad, will ya?" Donald Duk asks his Uncle Donald Duk in his nicest, most sincere voice.

A faint light soaks through the thin curtains in the front room and stains the darkness with a sickly glow. Donald can now see a little by this dead light. Donald wants his eyes to take more time getting used to the dark. His uncle is not moved by a sweet voice, a polite manner. The old man's black eyes glower. Donald Duk does not want those eyes to see him and steps back.

"Your Baba is like my little son. You want me to help you lie to your father?"

"Not a lie. It won't hurt him."

"You burned his Black Tornado."

"He won't miss it. He'll think it . . . it got lost."

"You don't know the 108 heroes of *The Water Margin,* do you?" Uncle Donald says, smiling and glowering at the same time.

"*What* do you mean?"

Uncle Donald Duk leans back in his chair and laughs low enough not to wake anyone sleeping in the rooms down the hall. "The Water Margin is a place in China, kid. It's a huge swamp and marshland about the size of Rhode Island. It's kind of like the Okefenokee or the Everglades. You ever hear about those places, kid? I don't see any recognition light up in your eyes."

"Recognition?"

"You ask your teachers about the Okefenokee in Georgia and the Everglades in Florida. Ask them about what they call the Seminole Indians. Ha ha ha." Donald Duk is a large pudgy man. He wears a beard that is neither short nor long. "How can I tell you about *The Water Margin* if you don't know nothing? Hmm. Do you know the story of Robin Hood? Maybe you seen the movie with the star Errol Flynn. They show it all the time on the Disney Channel. I know you get cable TV, so you can catch the movie even if you have never seen it before. That movie was made before your daddy was born, and still you can see it, good as new. Shortcut to history."

"I know Robin Hood. Everybody's talking about Robin Hood these days."

"Good for you. So you know what Sherwood Forest is, right?"

"That's where the good farmers and Robin Hood hide out and become the Merry Men, who rob from the rich and give to the poor."

"Yeah. The Water Margin was a place like that. In the middle of the swamp there's a mountain. Mount Leongshan. Bad government just like *Robin Hood.* Bad guys in charge of the works. All the good guys who want better government are badmouthed by the guys in charge, and they go outlaw and hide out or get killed. Just like Robin Hood. But in the Chinese book, there are 108 Robin Hoods. They all lead gangs that have hideouts all over, and they all come together in one super gang and build a city of outlaws and huge stronghold on Mount Leongshan, in the middle of the Water Margin. Every Chinese boy and girls knows those 108 Robin Hoods like you know Robin Hood and his Merry Men. Little John, Friar Tuck and all them guys.

"One of those 108 Chinese Robin Hoods is a hood name of Lee Kuey. Nickname: the Black Tornado. His skin is so what they call *ruddy* they call Lee Kuey black. He is not too smart. He gets mad very easily. When he gets very mad, he takes off all his clothes. He goes naked and runs into a fight with a thirty-pound battle-axe in each hand. He loves to fight and kill people. When he runs out of the other side of a battle, his body is covered with layers of other people's drying blood. Kind of sickening, huh? But he's got principles. Ha ha!" Uncle Donald Duk laughs, catching the look on little Donald Duk's face. He laughs again.

"Here's a flash for you, kid. I know how that snooty private school you go to has pulled the guts out of you and turned you into some kind of engineer of hate for everything Chinese, but your real name is your Chinese name. And your Chinese name is not Duk, but Lee. Lee, just like Lee Kuey. I myself have performed the role of the fierce and terrifying Black Tornado many times on the stage of the Cantonese opera. I myself made that plane you stole to fly and burn all by your selfish little self over Chinatown. Now you ask me to keep it secret. You think your daddy won't notice one little plane is missing from his dining room sky? Ha! He will notice it! He will expect me to notice it. He will expect me to get red in the face and demand some explanation."

Uncle Donald stares a hole through little Donald Duk faster than little Donald can dodge. "I don't need any explanation from you. You hate your name. You blame every Chinese who ever lived, everything Chinese you ever heard of for the way white kids act like fools when they hear your name. You don't look too happy to hear your most famous ancestor is one bloodthirsty homicidal maniac.

"Hey, I'll tell you this much, kid. There are stories in *The Water Margin* about our ancestor that will hit you like a kick in the stomach and make you sick! I can tell them to you, but I don't want to give you bad dreams."

"I already have bad dreams."

"Bad dreams! About what, kid?" Uncle Donald Duk asks, and Donald might be dreaming this. Donald Duk has been here before. He is no longer afraid. The plane is a long long time ago. "The old railroad," he says. "I like trains. I always liked trains."

"Your great-great-grandfather was the first of our Lees to come over from China. He worked on the Central Pacific when it went east over the Sierra and on to Promontory." Uncle Donald stops and sighs. "Did you ever see that old photograph of the Golden Spike Ceremony, where the C.P. Huntington and the Jupiter are cowcatcher to cowcatcher?"

"Yeah. People all over the locomotives waving their hats . . ."

"Did you ever wonder why there are no Chinese in that picture? Your great great-granddaddy and lots of other Chinese were there. So why don't you find a picture of your great-great-granddaddy there? But here in this old railroad book of your daddy's . . ." He opens a book and says, "Go ahead, turn on the light, kid."

It is a winter scene. Chinese with long-handled shovels, sledge-hammers and pickaxes stand in the snow. Black pants. Black *minop* jackets. Black flat-brimmed, crowned hats. Black work boots. A white gang foreman on horseback wears a high-crowned, rolled, brimmed hat and a puffy hairy fur coat. Uncle Donald Duk points to a smiling Chinese face in the photo. "Look at how young we were when we came to build the railroad. Look at that kid. He's on foot in the snow, and smiling. He can't be more than sixteen. Your great-great-granddaddy was even younger than that. More like your age, kid. How old are you now? Eleven? Twelve?"

Donald Duk has never seen this book before. He has never seen this old photograph before. He has been there. His feet say so. He recognizes the snow. It is the first winter the Chinese will spend in the mountains. Donald turns to go to his room and continue into the dream he knows is waiting for him. Uncle Donald's voice emerges inside Donald Duk's mood. "Just a minute. Tomorrow. You will tell your father what you did with the little plane. And you will offer to build the replacement in time for the flying and burning of all 108 off Angel Island. Your daddy will ask my permission, since I built the model in the first place. Of course, I will say it is okay with me."

4

PERHAPS DONALD DUK is too anxious to get to sleep and dream.
The other nights the dreams come, they are all bad because they
are all about Chinese he does not understand. Now he wants to
dream for a look at his great-great-grandfather. He counts it off on
his fingers before his eyes. The father of the father of the father of
the father. Great-great-grandfather. Four generations. He is the
fifth. Five generations ago. Five Duks or Lees ago, a relative is
young and working on the transcontinental railroad, from the
west end of the line. "Okay, I'll tell him. Okay. I'll build it." Donald Duk says to his Uncle Donald and finally is alone in the dark
of the hallway. He walks in the dark to his room.

The dream comes on like a movie all over his eyes. The Chinese
are all young. The Chinese gold-rush miners buy their black
denim jeans and high-top leather workboots and black felt hats
from a Chinese store in Sacramento. Some hold up their black
denim pants with both suspenders and wide black leather belts.
These are the powderboys, the blasters who pack the powder and
shove the detonators down the holes drilled into the rock. The
sure-handed, wiry and quick-muscled young of all these China-

man boys playing with dynamite and granite is no laughing matter. And here he is, the first Lee of the famly in America, scooting down the face of a sheer granite mountain before the dynamite blows. Twelve years old.

Hey, I'm only twelve. How do I eat! I don't know how to cook for myself. Don't panic. Go with the flow. We're all hungry. It's suppertime in the Sierra. On the edge of our camp is a camp of Chinese businesses on wheels. Each wagon is owned and operated by a lone man, married couple or small family that specializes in making a Cantonese pastry, a meal in a bun, soup in a bowl. There are herbalists ready to diagnose and prescribe herbal mixtures to remedy most ailments. It is like a convention of ice cream trucks and taco stands on wheels, except these move very slowly and are parked most of the time.

Whole families live out of the wagons. In front of the wagons they have unpacked the woks and cooking tools, and built their stoves and ovens. Tables and counters, ceramic bowls and spoons, flags and signs are all set out. The life around every wagon looks like the life inside a house with all the walls gone.

The front of the wagons are arranged in a semicircle behind the railroad camp. These people and their food follow the Chinese building the railroad across the mountains and keep them fed through three winters. Two of them are very hard winters. One winter they all live in wooden tunnels they built to shelter the tracks. The snowsheds are buried in snow. Beyond the snowsheds they live in tunnels carved in deep frozen snow.

Along the way some wagons drop out and others drop in. Babies are born along the way. Sometimes someone dies. They are buried not far from where they drop. Today before twilight a wagon backs into place. The horses are set out to graze. The sun is still up, but already the camp is in the shadows of the mountains they have taken years to cross.

The back of the new wagon drops, and a man in opera costume steps onto a little stage. "I am Yin the handsome. Yin the singer!

Yin the magician! Yin the elf! In my hand is an exact replica of Kwan Kung's halberd. The god of fighters and writers himself designed, forged and named his weapon *The Black Dragon Doh!* It weighs more than one hundred pounds!" He throws it out into the crowd! Ho! A young man catches it and . . . cannot hold it—it is too heavy—and drops it to the ground with a clang and a thud. It raises a cloud of dust. "Come on, hand it back up here, boys. Two or three of you guys should be able to do it. Come on. They tell me you boys are strong and fit who work on the railroad."

Three men in the crowd grunt and lift the halberd off the ground and heave it up to the costumed man on the little stage. He grabs the halberd by the long shaft with one hand and hoists it upright. A huge blade that looks like the cheapest kind of can opener but huge sits at the top of a long iron pole. The bottom of the pole is a pike, designed to poke holes through armor and break the ribs of horses. The costumed man twirls the halberd that three men had struggled with. He twirls it over his head, behind his back, between his legs. His son throws a huge chunk of wood off the end of the wagon, scattering the crowd. The costumed man jumps off the stage twirling the halberd, swings and whacks the rolling chunk of wood from every direction till there's nothing but splinters on the ground. He twirls the halberd from hand to hand and lets it twirl around and go blade-first chunk into the ground. The blade is so heavy it chops into the hard ground up to its shank before it stops.

"You wonder at my strength! I do not pretend to have the strength of Kwan Kung. But I do drink this kung fu brew every day, and you see for yourself, Kwan Kung's weapon seems made for my hands. How about a couple of you boys twisting that thing out of the ground for me and handing it back up?"

He sets the halberd aside and introduces his son. A twelve-year-old boy. He has been training since he could roll over. He has been adding the family kung fu brew to his food since before he could chew.

Suddenly the halberd is alive again in the man's hand. It twirls up and out of his hand down into the twelve-year-old boy's, where it stays alive. The boy throws the halberd to his mother. Mother and son flash through the moves of a kung fu fight. Bare hands fight the halberd. One steals the halberd from the other and the fight goes on. As they fight, the costumed man hawks bottles of his kung fu brew.

"Get your strength together, focus your energy, boys, you're going to need it. You remember a few years ago, on the other side of the mountains, you laid almost five miles of straight rail in one day. And the Central Pacific said it was a world's record. Sure, you do. You got to watch the chief engineer, owners and reporters drink champagne under a tent the next week to celebrate. Well, the Irish Union Pacific crews said they were going to lay ten miles of track in one day and invited the Central Pacific bigshots to watch. The Union Pacific boys huffed and puffed all day, and spiked down only six and four-tenths miles of track."

"We have been averaging six and seven-tenths of a mile a day since we came out of the mountains," someone says.

"The Union Pacific is betting the Central Pacific $10,000 they can lay more track in one twenty-four-hour day than you boys."

"They are?"

"Them Irish are big and strong, boys. They have a fire in their bellies and a glint in their eyes. They hate you Chinamans and know their cause is righteous. They are praying to their God. They are praying to their Virgin Mary. They plan to work as many of the twenty-four hours a day has as they can. They say Chinese are too little to make ten miles of track fast to the ground in a straight line in one day. They say the Chinese are smaller and poop out sooner than big white men, with big hearts that don't poop out as fast as little hearts. I tell you, boys, my family's kung fu brew will not let you poop out."

The kid glimpses an eye on him. Another kid inside the wagon peeks out from behind the little curtain that serves as a backdrop to the little stage. A twin! A twelve-year-old girl joins her brother and father on stage and catches the twirling halberd. She is so pretty! He wouldn't mind talking to her. It seems she wouldn't mind talking to him.

Donald Duk wakes up! The dream was so real. Her eyes were happy to see him. He wants to stay asleep and dream he is a powderboy, taking to prying iron and spiking rail across Nevada, and never wake up. That's why he wakes up fast and is happy to hear the double-stringed fiddle singing throaty and shrill out in the street, in the real world. Even it that real world is nothing but Chinatown.

5

DAD WAKES UP EARLY every morning to go out shopping for his restaurant. Sometimes Mom and the twins go with him, and Dad buys everyone breakfast at Uncle's Café on Clay Street. This morning Dad wakes everyone up early. The air is still dark blue outside and looks cold. "It is the first day of the first month of the Chinese New Year of the Rooster, boys," Dad says. "Get dressed in your best clothes and shine your shoes. We have to do a little early business. Fish don't celebrate the New Year, so fishermen and people who pride themselves on fresh fish in the evening must devise means to live real life without committing great offense to the expression of an ideal."

"What does that mean?"

"It means we get down to the market early, we make our buy of fish, we get to the butcher and the vegetable man and make our buys for the day, done early. The rest of the morning we look like everyone else taking a day off in our best clothes. Enjoy the morning of the first morning of the Chinese New Year, boys and girls! Hurry up! Get washed. Get dressed! And let's get out!"

Uncle Donald Duk has new Chinese silk jackets for everyone.

He even has one for Arnold. He gives the twins jackets of two different colors so he can tell them apart, he says and laughs. It is early morning laughter. Not too loud. Not too hard. Venus Duk wears the red jacket. Penelope Duk wears the green.

Uncle Donald Duk does not say a word about late last night. He does not mention planes or walk into the dining room or shoot sharp looks into Donald Duk's eyes. He does not have to say anything to Dad right now. Not yet. And he doesn't.

When? The first day of Chinese New Year is a holiday for Chinese in San Francisco. He does not have to go to school. Arnold is staying out with him. Mom asks why Dad is shopping for the restaurant. "Isn't the restaurant closed for the first day?"

"The first day is for the close family, Ah-Arnold," Dad says, adding the "Ah" in front of everyone's name, the way Chinese do. "That is why Donald's mom is right. The restaurant is closed. But my close family is larger because of you and Uncle Donald Duk.

"You see, I am opera people. Uncle Donald Duk is my *sifu*. My teacher. His opera company is opera people from all over the world. They came here special to perform in Chinatown this Chinese New Year. So they are all my close family this year."

"Ah-King! That's thirty people!"

"Fifty," Dad says. "They have a troupe of children with the company. Some are the children of old opera families and eat like monsters."

"So you are going to be busy all day in the restaurant kitchen preparing a banquet for fifty," Mom says. "That is a lot of close family, Uncle Donald."

"Let's see. Actually, it's more like 150, Mommy," Uncle Donald Duk says.

"Uncle Donald Duk!" Mom says and looks angry. The twins giggle and snort.

"Hey! I'm going to help Daddy cook, Mommy! I'll be a good boy!" Uncle Donald Duk says.

"Me too!" says Venus.

"You're a good boy?" asks Penelope.

"No! I'm going to cook with Daddy in the big kitchen."

"And me!" Penelope says.

"How about you, Arnold?" Venus asks.

"Cooking with our dad is so much fun!" Penelope says.

"Wait till you hear him yell!" Venus says.

"You know how to cook, too?" Arnold asks Uncle Donald Duk.

"You want to be able to take care of yourself, kid, you have to know how to cook. You stick with me, you'll be okay."

"I thought we were going to build model planes after we got back," Arnold says. Donald does not want to talk about model airplanes right now. Arnold does not know how close he is to getting Donald Duk in trouble. And Donald can't tell him.

Uncle Donald pats Arnold on the back. "Don't worry, kid. We will. Then we'll go down to the restaurant later. Don't worry."

Tonight in the restaurant Donald will tell Dad about the little plane. How it flew. How it burned. Dad will be with his opera teacher and his opera people. They will be drinking some. They will be happy. Dad will not want them to see him whacking his son on the butt. He will have to take the news without going crazy and getting too loud. That seems a good plan, Donald Duk thinks.

Out on the street in the early morning shadows of Chinatown, Arnold Azalea is startled by the noise. Chinatown in the morning is hard on the ears of a boy used to hearing the empty spaces between the trees. From Donald Duk's apartment you can hear rush hour roar into being on the freeway. Cars howl out of the Broadway tunnel and snarl and growl in stops and starts toward the on-ramp to freeways to everywhere. The regular, rhythmic rise and flow of rush hour motors muttering up to and away from the three stoplights through Chinatown wake Arnold up every night he stays over. He is not used to the noise.

"Remember that *Huckleberry Finn* we read in class? I think the rolling tires on Broadway and the freeway sound like big water rolling in a river," Donald Duk says. Uncle Donald Duk chuckles, and zap goes a memory. Last year or the year before, when Donald can't stand the noise in the morning, one morning, one Chinese New Year, Uncle Donald Duk tells him to listen to the traffic like a river flowing by. Like water. "Sometimes it's fast. Sometimes it's slow. Sometimes it floods. Sometimes it dries up."

"Here, boys," Uncle Donald Duk says in his big voice. In his hand he holds two little red envelopes with a design printed in gold on them. Donald takes an envelope. "Here, you too, kid," Uncle Donald Duk's big voice booms off all the tile in the fish store.

"Take it," Donald Duk whispers to his friend.

"What is it?" Arnold asks out loud. And Donald Duk is embarrassed. He feels his ears turn very hot and almost hurt. It is not his friend embarrassing him, Donald Duk tells himself. It is not Arnold's fault he does not know what *lay see* is. It is Uncle Donald Duk's fault for making Arnold look like a little fool in the first place.

"Don't you know what *lay see* is?" Venus asks and giggles.

Penelope pulls a brand new folded-up piece of paper money out of the envelope. She unfolds it and squeals, "Oooh, fifty dollars!"

"Where are your manners, girls!" Mom sings in a snooty British accent from an old Alec Guinness movie on TV that makes her remember when she was a girl. "You should whisper! And wait till Uncle Donald Duk's back is turned, at least!"

"Yeeee! Mom! Not in front of Uncle Donald Duk!" Venus says.

"And give it back. It's too much!"

"Ah-Daisy! Your boy's number-twelve year! All of you keep it! I am a member of the family. Ah-King ahhh, didn't you say I was your family? Yes or no? So you keep it, you twins. Hey, kid, you want to know what this is?"

"His name is Arnold. Don't call him *kid!* . . . Please don't call him *kid.*"

"Hey, Ah-Arnold ahhh. This is called *lay see.* It means, oh, *'lucky money.'* At New Year's time, the old Chinese give *lay see* to the kids. It means we wish when you grow up you get married and be as happy as we old farts are."

"Give it back, ladies," Mom says. "Uncle Donald Duk is not married, so his *lay see* doesn't mean anything."

"I still want them to be as happy as I am! Keep it."

"That's what I'm afraid of," Mom says.

Uncle Donald Duk laughs. "Okay, okay! Hey, Ah-Arnold, you keep it. She is just being polite. Now, everybody just be polite, stop fussing and put it in your pocket. This morning you are going to hear lots of people saying *Goong hay fot choy* and *Ho see fot choy*. It's our Chinese way of saying Happy New Year to each other. Okay, Arnold?"

"Okay, *Goong hay fot choy,*" Arnold says. Donald Duk taught his friend how to say *Goong hay fot choy* weeks ago. Mr. Meanwright made Donald Duk walk to the front of the room and teach all twenty students in his history class how to say *Goong hay fot choy*. Mr. Meanwright lived for a year in China. He studied kung fu in Chinatown. Mr. Meanwright speaks Mandarin, the Chinese national dialect.

A hundred years ago, all the Chinatowns in America were Cantonese. They spoke Cantonese. The only Chinese Donald has any ears for is Cantonese. Donald does not like the history teacher, Mr. Meanwright. Mr. Meanwright likes to prove he knows more about Chinese than Donald Duk. Donald Duk doesn't care. He knows nothing about China. He does not speak Mandarin. He does not care a lot about Chinatown either, but when Mr. Meanwright talks about Chinatown, Donald Duk's muscles all tighten up, and he wants Mr. Meanwright to shut up. Donald Duk gets away on Fred Astaire's dance steps. The old black-and-white musicals that were already old when Mom and Dad saw them in art houses seem as far from Chinatown, Chinese, the name Donald Duk as Donald Duk can get.

"*Goong hay fot choy! Goong hay fot choy! Ho see fot choy! Ho see fot choy!*" echoes in strange stereo down the empty street.

"Oh, no! It's the Frog Twins!" Donald Duk says, "Hide! Everybody, hide!"

"Cool it!" Dad growls under his breath, as Arnold is about to ask something. "Be cool and be nice, boys. We're going to visit the Fong Fong sisters tomorrow."

"What?" Donald Duk protests, "I don't believe it!"

"I said, cool it," Dad says.

"Are we really visiting the Fong twins tomorrow?" Donald Duk stretches his neck and whispers as loud as he can.

"The first day of the New Year is for close family. The second day you visit your . . ."

". . . poor relations," Donald Duk says, finishing Dad's thought.

Dad flicks his hand and raps Donald Duk on the back of his head with a knuckle. The knuckle goes "kawk" against Donald Duk's skull.

Ow! The hurt goes fast right through his head. Donald Duk blinks. He can't see! He can see. Whew! Okay.

"Be cool," Dad says. Donald Duk is cool.

"Goong hay fot choy! Goong hay fot choy!" the Frog Twins say. Even in their finest clothes they look like they are wearing everything they own. They wear glasses with large, thick round lenses that make their bulging eyes bulge out even more. They scare Donald Duk and make him laugh at the same time because they look like some popeyed goldfish his sisters have in their aquarium. What are the Frog Twins doing up this early in the morning?

"We were waiting for you," one Frog Twin says. "We're so happy we found you." They pat the twins and Donald Duk on the head.

"Goong hay fot choy," Dad says. "Have you eaten yet?"

"Oh, please, you are too generous," one says. "We want to especially wish your children Happy New Year," the other twin says. They are not carrying shopping bags today. They each carry one red plastic bag with red envelopes of *lay see.*

"Thank your aunties and wish them *Goong hay fot choy,"* Mom says with a smile in her voice.

"Goong hay fot choy," Venus and Penelope Duk say.

"Happy New Year," Donald Duk says.

"Such polite children!" one of the Frog Twins says. The other says, "And so clever!" They both pat Donald Duk on the head. Donald Duk does not like them patting him on the head. "How old will you be this year, boy?"

"Tell your aunties," Mom says.

"Twelve," Donald says."

"Just say *sup yee,*" Penny says.

"I can say *twelve* in Chinese by myself, if I want to."

"Oh, sure!" Venus says.

"Then say it!" Penelope chirps. "*Sup yee,* sir."

"Oooh, twelve!" one Frog Twin says. "Do you know what day today is?" the other says. "The first day of the Chinese New Year."

"Do you know what the seventh day of the Chinese New Year is?" one Frog Twin asks. And the other grins with her mouth open, looking like she's holding her breath.

"No," Donald says.

"Everybody's birthday!" the other Frog Twin says, and breathes again.

"Everybody's birthday? What does that mean?"

"Look for us then," one Frog Twin says.

"We'll be looking for you!" the other says. They wobble away arm in arm, giggling.

Donald Duk opens his eyes wide as surprise and asks, "I wonder if they have any hair under those funny hats. Some old Chinese women get bald just like old Chinese men."

"Oh, Little Donald!" Venus says, and bats him on the back of the head with her fingertips. "You really are too old for that tacky cute-kid act. Even if we are taller than you."

"That's because you are so much older, sisters dear," Donald singsongs.

"Tacky tacky tacky!" Penelope says.

"Girls and boys! All of you! This is the first day of the new year. Just for today, let's do everything right, okay?" Dad says. "I don't want any fighting. I don't want any messing with each other, understand?"

"Tell them!" Donald Duk nods toward his sisters. "They're older, they're supposed to be responsible for little me."

Oops, let the twins go. Donald Duk wants to disappear in front of his father. Does this game the twins play mean they know he flew and burned the plane? They skipped grades and got into high school young. They are in a gifted drama class where they learn to play mind games.

"Wow, fourteen already," Venus says. "I feel positively senile with responsibility."

"Donald is first son, huh, Daddy?" Penny says. "Tell your son, someday all of this will be his. We are merely daughters."

"Don't worry, girls, if no one comes by offering me just the right buffalo and pony for you, some of this will be yours too when I go," Dad says.

"Oh, Ah-King, the way you talk!" Mom hits Dad on his arm with her fist. Not hard.

"What if we marry rich, Daddy?" Venus asks.

"If you get married and nobody give me a buffalo and pony, you still get it, if I got it, when I go, okay?"

"And Donald will be taller than us by then and have no excuse not to be responsible," Penny says.

Did anything Dad and the twins just say mean they know the little open cockpit low-wing monoplane with cute wheelpants is missing and what Donald did to it? Donald is not sure. Is Dad giving him a chance to tell all, come clean, get it off his chest?

6

BEFORE FIRST LIGHT the first delivery trucks hush up on their air-brakes with the first fish, live crabs and clams. The fish are silent. The clatter of crab legs crawling over crabshells can't be heard very far down the street. It is the unlatching of the doors, the sliding of the doors in the steel tracks that sound like an auto wreck and pop his thought and scare the hair out of his head. Donald Duk's dad and Uncle Donald Duk lead the family past the dark closed curio shops, into a live fish store. All the clerks wear black rubber boots under their smocks and rubber aprons. They have not set out the shaved ice and arranged their fish in piles yet. The old ceramic tile floor and window counters are still dry. The walls are made of the same little eight-sided white bathroom tiles as the floor and counters. The whole fish store makes Donald think of a huge bathroom.

As Dad talks with the fish man, all the clerks go up to Uncle Donald Duk and shake his hand. He does not tell them about last night and the little model plane. The fish man laughs with Dad. Not a word from Dad about the P-26A that is not hanging from the dining room ceiling anymore. The clerks squish back and forth in their big rubber boots on the tile floor and empty several buckets of shaved ice onto the sloping tile shelves in the display window.

Next they unload giant clams. They have large shells, the size
and shape of a small loaf of French bread. A round thick tube of
flesh sticks out of the shell. "Ugh! Obscene!" Donald Duk says.

"What are they?" Arnold can't believe his eyes.

"Mmmmm! *Jerng putt fong!*" Venus yelps.

"Daddy! Get some for the banquet tonight!" Penelope picks up
the yelp where Venus leaves off.

"No!" Dad says.

"Please, Daddy," Venus says.

"We're not supposed to eat red meat, right?" Penelope gushes
wide-eyed. "And *jerng putt fong* is not red meat."

"Too common! A banquet is a banquet because all the food is
special, not common, nothing ordinary."

"Good," Donald Duk says. "I want a filet mignon wrapped in
bacon, with . . ."

Donald Duk is cut off by Dad, "No. Beef is common! It used to
pull wagons and plows. No. We don't eat work animals tonight."

"We eat pets!" Uncle Donald Duk says, and Mom and the twins
laugh, and all slap Uncle Donald Duk's sleeve.

"Uncle Donald!" Mom scolds. "We do not! What will Donald's
friend Arnold think?"

"If we don't eat pets at banquets, when do we eat them? What
do you think we eat at banquets? You think we shoot down wild
animals in the woods and jungles and bring them back here for a
banquet?"

"Well, yes!" Mom says. "The bird's nest for bird's nest soup is
from wild birds. The shark's fin for shark's fin soup is from wild
sharks."

"Hey, Ah-Arnold," Uncle Donald Duk booms. "You want to
know what those ugly-looking things are, right? *Jerng putt fong.*
We call them 'elephant trunk' because that is what they look like.
They are king clams from Seattle."

"And they're delicious!" Venus says.

"Common or not, they are just heaven when poached," Penelope says.

"Gee, that's just the way I like my heaven," Donald says.

"Oh, by the way," Dad says to the fish man, leaning his head in close to the man to speak privately. Donald wonders why Dad doesn't want him to hear and, so, listens. "You know those Fong Fong Twins. When you see them walk by, *give* them two two-pound catfish. Not one four-pound fish. They don't taste as sweet as the smaller ones, understand? That okay? And put it on my bill."

"Haa! Brother King, you come in here on the first day of the year and tell me my fish are not sweet?"

"Naw, I am not that way, brother. My good name among the great *sifu* of world cookery depends on you always having fish for all tastes," Dad smiles. "For all tastes. Send over forty large catfish to the restaurant day after tomorrow, for the traditional first night out of the year. And you come out for dinner with my family and the opera people, and I will make special for you a spicy salt-stuffed catfish nobody in the world makes but me."

"You're a very generous man," the fish man says.

"Yes, I am, if I say so myself. *Ho see fot choy,* my friend," and Dad shoves Donald and Arnold and the family out of the echoes and bright tile of the fish store into the morning growing on the streets of Chinatown. Restaurant owners, cooks and chefs from all over San Francisco are the only people on the street, now, like Dad, out buying the freshest, the sweetest, the most crisp fish and Chinese vegetables for the day's business.

The sun rises in the east. Just west of Chinatown are two of San Francisco's famous hills. Much of the morning Chinatown sits cool in the dissolving pool of fog and shadows of Nob Hill and Russian Hill. This morning as the rush hour passes and the traffic settles to a pleasant roar, the streets of Chinatown are crowded. But the people out walking this morning are not shopping. More men than usual wear hats. And the hats they wear are fine felt hats. The curio shops are closed. The supermarkets, butcher shops and fish stores are closed, but ready to open in the afternoon. Families are out for a walk on the first morning of the year in their best clothes and best moods. The fingernails are cleaned, the shoes shined, and small children dressed in Chinese silk robes, long vests, slippers and hats.

Everywhere families stop on the street, shake hands and give each other's children the red envelopes of *lay see*. They tell their children to say thank you and wish auntie and uncle *Goong hay fot choy* or *Ho see fot choy*, and one family politely asks the other if they have eaten yet, and the other politely refuses, and they all move on down the street until they get hungry and walk into one of the many open hot Hong Kong style *deem sum* shops for lunch.

When Mom and Dad run out of the red envelopes of *lay see* they packed, Mom asks the twins for a few of their envelopes.

"Not the *lay see* Uncle Donald Duk gave us!" Venus says.

"Of course not," says Penelope.

"Isn't that bad luck or something?" Arnold asks Donald on the sly. And Uncle Donald Duk grins. He has ears like radar.

"Bad luck?" says Uncle Donald. "Oh, no. Everybody ends up giving out some of the *lay see* their kids got. We can talk back and forth for another hour maybe, and someone will give us some *lay see* we probably gave somebody else. No problem. It's not a super-stition. It's something we like to do. That's all."

"Ten years ago, the only people out today would be old, the last of the old immigrants. Right, Uncle Donald? Now, all these new immigrants from Indochina. Crowds. Whole families. China-town is jumping again. These people are doing what our great-grandparents did, back in the days of the gold rush and railroads."

"What's that, Mr. Duk?" Arnold asks.

"They are getting together clubs, family associations. People from the same county form an association. They are making tongs."

"The tongs were bad, weren't they?"

"Some good. Some bad. The good ones got together in a big alliance to stamp out the bad ones, making the Tong Wars. That was eighty years ago. I belong to one of the associations that belongs to that alliance of good tongs."

"Oh, the tongs are dinosaurs!"

"Dinosaurs? What do you mean, Little Donnie Duk?" Venus asks, all fake wonder.

"He means those ancient old tongs don't deserve to live," Penelope says.

"Hey, everybody's gotta give up the old and become American. If all these Chinese were more American, I wouldn't have all my problems," Donald Duk says, and whoops! He stops. And Dad is laughing. He's not mad. He's laughing. That makes Donald Duk mad.

"Why is Dad laughing, Little Donnie Duk wonders," Venus says, writing out loud again.

"Oh oh! Little Donnie Duk does not look happy," Penelope says.

"I think Donald Duk may be the very last American-born Chinese-American boy to believe you have to give up being Chinese to be an American," Dad says. "These new immigrants prove that. They were originally Cantonese, and did not want to be Chinese. When China conquered the south, these people went further south, into Vietnam, Laos, Cambodia, Thailand. They learned French. Now they're learning English. They still speak their Cantonese, their Chinese, their Viet or Lao or Cambodian, and French. Instead of giving anything up, they add on. They're including America in everything else they know. And that makes them stronger than any of the American-born, like me, who had folks who worked hard to know absolutely nothing about China, who believed that if all they knew was 100 percent American-made in the USA Yankee know howdy doodle dandy, people would not mistake them for Chinese."

"Mmm. Sounds like a little Donnie Duk we know."

How can Dad embarrass me so, in front of my white friend? Donald wants to know. He is shocked his father is talking to him this way. He is sure Dad is getting at him for burning his model plane. But Dad hasn't said so. So Donald Duk stays cool. No backtalk.

"You know what else, Ah-Arnold, my friend?" Uncle Donald Duk says. His voice is a cheerful whizz and whirr. "In the old days, when my family ran out of their own *lay see,* it was a sign it was time to go get lunch. And that's what I think, Ah-King. Time for lunch!"

7

THE RESTAURANT LOOKS A LITTLE like a nightclub in an old Fred Astaire musical. A wide staircase down to the dining room like in *Flying Down to Rio*. Stainless steel pillars. The waiters wear black tuxedo trousers, black vests over white shirts and black bowties. The owners of the restaurant wear white shirts and black bowties without the black vests. They rush up to Uncle Donald and shake his hand. They wish each other *ho see fot choy*. The owners look urgently for a table for Uncle Donald Duk's party. Do the owners know that Uncle Donald Duk's party is King Duk, Daisy Duk, Venus Duk, Penelope Duk, Donald Duk and his friend Arnold Azalea? If they know will they laugh?

Lunch! If Donald can get through lunch without Uncle Donald Duk betraying him or making Dad lose his temper, he won't have to see Dad till dinnertime. And if he goes to his tap dance class at the Chinese Fred Astaire's Chinatown Dance Studio, he will be late for dinner. Donald is thinking of a plan to get through the day without getting his feelings hurt when Arnold asks, "Mr. Duk, do you think I could make one of those stick-and-paper model airplanes while I'm staying over?"

Dad smiles, leans back in his chair and says, "You can't resist, can you? After seeing them up there awhile and seeing them wobble on the air when the window's open and a little breeze blows in off the bay, you have to make one. Daisy and the twins. It was the same. Venus saw how the light shines right through the paper skin and shows up the bones. In fact, Penelope can start you on a plane after lunch."

"My grandfather says he built stick-and-paper flying models too when he was a boy."

"Oh, yeah. This is the art of grandfathers when they were boys."

"He says the World War 1 biplanes were the best fliers. Do you think I could make a biplane?"

"Sure, but I don't think you'll have time to finish a biplane. You don't want to spend all your time cutting out little little pieces. How about this? The GeeBee Racer. An old Cleveland kit."

"Gramps says he used to like Cleveland kits the best."

Whose friend is Arnold anyway? Okay. Arnold in deep concentration cutting balsa wood with a razor knife will make it easier for Donald Duk to disappear off to his tap dance class. No one will notice him leaving. No one will miss him. Is that what he wants? One day they will look up and see him dancing in one of his old movies. "Oh, it's Fred Astaire!" they will say. "Why, he used to be Chinese from Chinatown. His name was Donald Duk then."

First comes the *ho see fot choy*. Arnold goodie-goods again! "Is that the same *ho see fot choy* that means Happy New Year?"

"You have good ears," Uncle Donald Duk says. "*Ho* is oysters. *See* is, what is it, Ah-King?"

"Bean vermicelli. A thin transparent noodle made out of beans. The *fot choy* is a casserole of reconstituted dried vegetables. *Ho see fot choy* sounds just like *ho see fot choy*. So the wish for a happy new year is a traditional new year's dish."

"Oh, yum yum!" the twins say at the second dish the waiters put on the table.

"Hey, Ah-Arnold," Dad says. "You were curious about the *jerng putt fong*. Well, here it is."

"What?"

"That king clam you saw at the fish market. You call them *Gooey* duck though you spell it g-e-o-d-u-k . Gee-oh duck clam. Eat it. It's good."

"It looks like the sole of my Reeboks sliced real real thin!" Donald Duk says, and laughs too loud. "Look at his face! He can't eat it."

"It's delicious!" Venus says.

"You take a piece with your chopstick and dip it in the secret sauce," Penelope says.

"What's so secret about it? Anybody can see it's just soy sauce, green onion, ginger, dried chili, oil, some sesame. Huh, Mommy?" Venus says.

"Whoa, listen to the Chinese Betty Crocker!" Penelope says.

"Ah! Twins! " Donald Duk says. "Don't you wish you had twin sisters, Arnold?"

"Look at this!" Dad says, "Ah-Arnold likes the *jerng putt fong!*"

Why is dad being so nice to Arnold? Is this Dad's way of saying he knows what Donald Duk did last night? "I thought *jerng putt fong* was too common for New Year," Donald Duk says.

"Take it easy," Uncle Donald Duk says and pats Donald Duk on the back. "It's too common for a banquet. This is lunch, not a banquet. Lunch is common food. The banquet—oh la la, as they say in France."

Lunch is going on forever. Donald stops talking. He won't give himself away.

The longer no one talks about last night and the little low-wing monoplane, the more dangerous the situation feels to Donald Duk.

Everyone in the restaurant seems to know Uncle Donald Duk. Everyone is so happy he is performing Cantonese opera in San Francisco this New Year. Everyone smiles and blushes and does little bows in front of Uncle Donald Duk as if he is a Hollywood star.

Donald Duk has ears. He hears what people say. He understands more Chinese by ear than he dares speak. In Canton, in China, Uncle Donald Duk is a star. In Hong Kong he was a big star after the Communists took over mainland China. To the Chinese all over the world, here in San Francisco, he is a star. So why is this Cantonese star here? Dad is his greatest student. Dad is a legend among the opera people all over the world. They tell stories of Dad helping any opera people passing through San Francisco.

When Dad was a fourteen-year-old boy, he ran away from home, the legend goes. He slipped into China and apprenticed himself to Uncle Donald. Does Donald dare run away from home to another country, another language? Dad can play Chinese, he can eat Chinese and go gah-gah over Chinese, but no matter what, he is white. He can leave Chinatown. He can leave the Chinese. He can go home to hear the spaces between the trees and never come back. All he has to do is cross the street. Dad's parents didn't want to be Chinese. Donald Duk doesn't want to be Chinese. Why does Dad like being Chinese? Doesn't he know everybody talks about him funny?

Back at home, Uncle Donald talks about what a wonderful opera performer Dad was. The twins cover themselves in smocks before sitting down to work on the balsa wood skeleton of their model plane. Uncle Donald wishes Dad would perform in this opera and show the actors and singers in his company real genius. Dad came home from Hong Kong and got a job as a brakeman on the Southern Pacific Railroad before he started cooking, Uncle Donald says.

"Daaaddy?" the twins say together in surprise.

"It's true," Mom says.

"He never talks about it," Venus says.

"Maybe it was a traumatic experience for him," Penelope says.

"He says all he learned on the railroad was the universal pronoun for everything on the railroad—*cocksucker,*"Mom whispers the word and goes instantly red in the face, even as she holds herself in a nonchalant and noble pose.

"Mom!" Venus wails. "Such talk!"

"Well, it's true! And that is probably why your father does not talk about the railroad," Mom says with mock haughtiness.

"You're still blushing, Mom," Penelope says low.

"How about you?" Uncle Donald Duk asks Donald Duk. "Your daddy wook onna Sudden Paciffee, you know dat?" he asks Donald Duk. Sometimes what Uncle Donald Duk says sounds diseased with a very Chinese accent and startles Donald. Is it his ears? Does Uncle Donald sound that way all the time?

No. Donald didn't know that.

The dining room table is extra large. It is covered with a four-foot wide and eight-foot long sheet of plywood subflooring. The family unfolds the model airplane plans and tacks them to the plywood. They cover the plans with waxed paper. They can see through the waxed paper to the plans. They pin and glue the light balsa wood parts over the plans. The model airplane cement does not stick to the waxed paper, so the glued parts do not get stuck to the paper plans when the glue dries. Mom takes a place at the table. She unpacks a Comet Models kit.

"Who are you making, Mom?" Venus, the first twin, asks.

"It's a P-38 Lightning. It says so right on the plans," Penelope says. Donald Duk cannot tell if they are making fun of each other sounding stupid or performing a stupid act for Arnold.

"I said *who* not *what*, stupid!" Venus says.

"You can't call me *stupid,* stupid! It's still the first day, remember," Penelope says.

"This is my sisters' Stupid Act," Donald mutters to Arnold.

"Mom, tell her to be cool and nice because it's the first day."

"Be cool and nice, ladies," Mom says. She smooths the waxed paper over the flattened plans. She tapes the corners of the waxed paper to the plywood.

"Say, Mom. Who are you making?" Penelope asks.

"Are you trying to shock Arnold, talking innuendo like that?" Venus asks her sister.

"We are supposed to feel confused in our puberty by this kind of talk," Donald says.

"Oh, this is going to be the great woman fighter called Ten Feet of Steel," Mom says. "She was her family's champion. Actually she was the general of a small army that protected her family domain. But after the army of the crooked government wiped out her small army and killed her father, she joins the outlaws of Leongshan Marsh. She is called Ten Feet of Steel because she fights with two five-foot-long swords."

"Wow!" the twins say together.

"Ten Feet of Steel charges into battle with her horse's reins between her teeth and one of her swords in each hand. She can carve her way through a thousand men. On foot she can fight off a thousand men."

"Wow!" the twins say.

"She sounds like she could hold off a thousand men with the smell of her sweat," Donald Duk says.

"Oh, stop bugging us!" the twins say together, as if they say this often.

"Bug bug bug bugbugbugbug . . ." Donald Duk says, but Arnold does not join him. Arnold does not laugh. Arnold is all eyes on Mom's hands and the plans. Good. No one looks up at the empty place in the toy sky.

"All right, Arnold. You watch me. I will start building this P-38 and you watch. You cut the bulkheads and these things for the wings out with this razor knife. And the little slots where the sticks fit in, you file out with this little file I made with sandpaper and a bit of balsa wood. See? Just the right size." As she talks, she moves the knife into the wood like she is drawing with a pencil. "This balsa wood is very soft, and it breaks oh so easily. So you have to use sharp blades all the time, and you have to be very sure and be very careful."

"You look like you're cutting it very fast, Mrs. Duk," Arnold says so sweetly and nicely Donald Duk wants to go pukey on the table. But he curls his toes inside his shoes and cools it.

"Well, I have been building model airplanes since I was a little girl," Mom says. "I just love it when they fly. They look so real. And they don't look real at all. Their flight is like magic."

"Oh, Mom! How positively Existential! Gee!" Venus says.

"Yeah, Mom, that's so fifties Zen angst! Yeeeeh!" Penelope says.

At exactly the same time, the twins are ready to attach the wings to the round cigar-shaped bodies of their planes. They are both making identical models of the stub-winged GeeBee Racer.

"Okay, Arnold," Mom says, "we don't need another GeeBee Racer. So you just watch me now. In about an hour, I have to go down to the restaurant and help out Uncle King, and then you can finish Ten Feet of Steel." Mom has Arnold calling her Auntie Daisy. He calls Dad, Uncle King. Donald Duk wants to call the loony bin and have all of Chinatown hauled away.

Larry Louie's second-story dance studio looks out over Clay Street and a Chinatown alley. Gold letters printed on his large windows spell out:

Larry Louie
"The Chinese Fred Astaire"
DANCE INSTRUCTION
Group — Private
Tap — Jazz — Modern
Latin — Flamenco

LARRY LOUIE IS AN OLD MAN. He stays thin trying to look like Fred Astaire. He dyes his thin hair black. The thin skin of his scalp shines through the thin stripes of his greased and combed hair.

Up the stairs to the studio are old glossy photos of a young Larry Louie dancing in the spotlight at an old Chinatown nightclub during World War II. There are pictures of him posing with a movie camera and an all-Chinese camera crew. There is a picture of him in a bit part in a Frank Sinatra movie. A picture of him in an old episode of the *Ironside* TV police show. Donald Duk climbs the stairs past the photos. One old photo of Larry Louie on each side of every step up to the studio. The photos of him dancing in the spot at the old Forbidden City are the best. His face looks very Chinese in the photos, but young Larry Louie forty-eight years ago looks more like Fred Astaire than the old man does today. He plucks his eyebrows. He clips the springy hairs that grow out of his nose with fingernail clippers. Larry Louie likes to tell his classes all about himself. Donald really does not care. All he wants to do is dance.

Donald Duk does not respect Larry Louie at all. Larry Louie can teach Donald Duk the basic technique of tap dance. Donald Duk needs to learn the basics. He knows that. And Mom cannot get Dad to pay for lessons from anybody else. Teaching is all Larry Louie is good at. He does not want to look like Larry Louie when he is an old man. Larry Louie is a failure because he does not really want to be Fred Astaire. Donald Duk wants to be Fred Astaire.

At the top of the stairs. The studio looks empty. What? "Oh, Ah-Donald! I thought you understood. There is no class tonight. It is the first day of the first month of the new year."

"You look taller!" Donald Duk says, instead of saying he is wrong. He looks around the studio. The place feels strange. No class tonight? Then what is the Chinese with the guitar doing here? Who is that woman with the fringed shawl over her shoulders? Two are sitting. Larry Louie is standing and looking taller. Strange.

"I'm wearing my flamenco boots," Larry Louie says. "My friend, Mr. Yin is in town with the Cantonese opera. He is also a fine flamenco guitarist. He used to play for La Florita and myself thirty years ago. Are we really that old, my dears? So, while he is gracing Chinatown with his presence, we have been reviving *Los Chinos Gitanos.* "Larry Louie's voice, like his shiniest hairs, comes out of his nose.

"You are most welcome to stay. In a bit, we will be going to your father's restaurant for the family dinner, anyway, so we will all wind up in the same place, sooner or later. Do you know what flamenco is?" Larry Louie asks. "It used to be all around Chinatown. The Patio Andaluz. The Sinaloa Club. Carmen Amaya— Queen of the Gypsies, they called her—danced there. The Casa Madrid, the Old Spaghetti Factory on Green Street. La Bodega on Columbus. Oh, there used to be flamenco guitarists and dancers and singers all over residential Chinatown."

"Flamenco?"

"The music, song and dance of the Spanish gypsy, Donald. Unleashed passion and superhuman restraint. Pagan heat and passionate devotion to their God and El Señor." As Larry Louie talks he stretches his arms out in front of him and snaps his fingers. All his fingers snap a little popping sound off his thumbs. Donald Duk hates it when he talks in rhythm and tries to dance. The talk sounds stupid and messes up the dance. But the rhythm he's snapping with his fingers and stamping with his feet can't be messed up.

Mr. Yin doesn't seem to speak. He plays the guitar like nothing Donald Duk has ever heard. And La Florita, the woman in the shawl, is clapping her hands. Each clap sounds like a snapping twig. She claps fast bursts of crunchy claps.

Why does a Cantonese opera musician play Spanish gypsy guitar? Why does Larry Louie, the Chinese Fred Astaire, dance flamenco for fun?

"Out of respect," Larry Louie says. Mr. Yin still plays. Larry Louie moves his arms and hands to the guitar as he talks. "Back in the fifties, after that Korean War, some of us thought about being a minority race. Now, the gypsies in Spain can be called an oppressed minority race. But the gypsies are not living their lives, laying their deaths or making their music on the doorstep of their oppressors. All the white people in Spain could die right now, and the flamenco would still be flamenco. The gypsies are still gypsies. You can hear and feel the integrity in their music. I love it, don't you, Mr. Yin?" Mr. Yin's reply is a flurry of tinkly glassy notes and explosions of jackhammered chords.

"Wong Chew Mo introduced the American cowboy hat, bullwhip and sixgun to the Cantonese opera. The opera orchestra now includes the Hawaiian twangy guitar, European violin and saxophone. It seems only natural for Mr. Yin to introduce flamenco guitar into the Cantonese opera. The crashing pulses of rhythm, the shrill and tinkly flights of melody and moments of rhythmic senseless violence in flamenco and Cantonese opera are the same.

Philosophically though, they are not the same. I love and respect Fred Astaire. He's one of my idols. But, he was too light on his feet for a flamenco dancer. Too outgoing and shiny. I respect Fred Astaire. I enjoy trying to understand his dance by playing his old music and doing his old routines, step for step. And the same with flamenco. The steps of Vicente Escudero, Carmen Amaya, Jose Greco, Cruz Luna. Dancing flamenco, you don't feel anything like Fred Astaire."

Step by step. That's how he teaches people to dance like Fred Astaire. Step by step through the old routines. The fun is dancing to the old movie on Larry Louie's wall-sized screen. He talks about buying the old Fred Astaire movies on videocassette and a big-screen TV, but Donald Duk likes the movies. Donald Duk likes the sound of the projector behind the screen. Donald Duk is not sure he likes the flamenco. It's noisy. The stamp of the feet bounce out of the floor up into his legs, into his stomach and bump his heart. The guitar is not soft, not playing pretty sounds. It sounds like it will break. Mr. Yin looks like he doesn't hear all the noise his hands are making with the guitar in his lap. Mr. Yin looks like a zombie.

Larry Louie is nothing to be scared of. He is an old broken-down failure. It's the music, the guitar, the woman clapping and shouting things in Spanish that confuse Donald Duk and make Larry Louie's flamenco look dangerous, unpredictable and something Donald wants to do.

It might be the way Mr. Yin plays the guitar, but no matter how fast and bright he plays, the feeling of the sound is always dark and lowdown, too sullen and grouchy and nasty for Fred Astaire. Wherever Donald Duk is tired and cold, that's where the sound gets inside him and trembles.

All the while, watching these thin and aging Chinese make like a *cuadro* flamenco, Donald Duk thinks of the time he has left to tell Dad about last night. It is already the dark of another night, and he has not kept his promise to Uncle Donald Duk. Does he have to keep his promise to Uncle Donald Duk?

Sooner or later Donald Duk has to walk with the greasy Larry Louie, the strange La Florita, and Mr. Yin carrying his guitar through Chinatown to his father's restaurant for dinner. The evenings cool fast in San Francisco at this time of year.

"You don't recognize me, do you," Mr. Yin says. Donald Duk does not recognize him. A few steps down the street Donald Duk still does not recognize Mr. Yin. "I am your tai chi instructor at the White Crane Club."

"Oh!" Donald Duk stops in his tracks and takes another look. Does he hate the Chinese so much he doesn't look at them anymore? "When Larry Louie said you are with the Cantonese opera, I didn't think . . ." He didn't bother looking.

"No, it isn't your fault you didn't recognize me," Mr. Yin says. There's a twinkle in his voice. He laughs between his words. "I cast a spell on you."

"Oh, you are a musician and a magician too," Donald Duk says, then flash! Last night. Uncle Donald Duk watches Donald Duk take the plane down from the ceiling, and Donald Duk doesn't see him. A spell? "I didn't want you to see me," Uncle Donald Duk says. Donald Duk has eyes on him, and ears waiting on him. He has to say something. "I remember now! You're the one they call Yin the wrestler, Yin the music man, Yin the elf." No, that's the dream. That's where Donald Duk remembers seeing Mr. Yin last. In the dream.

"Oh, you're too kind," Mr. Yin says.

"Do you really play flamingo guitar in the opera?"

"Flamingo is a pink bird that stands on one leg in Florida," Mr. Yin says smiling and standing on one straight leg.

"I know what bird you're talking about!" Donald Duk says, hearing a strange squeak coming out of his mouth.

"You're growing up, young man," Larry Louie says, and both men hang soothing smiles and gooey good-doggie eyes on Donald Duk as if he's just wet his pants.

"I play flamenco guitar, and I play a number of Chinese instruments in the Cantonese opera, but gypsy flamenco guitar and

Cantonese opera? Hmmm. It is an idea, I suppose. I collect musicianship and the musical instruments of the world like your father collects the great cooking and cuisines of the world."

"You know my father's cooking?"

"Everybody knows your father's cooking. Only the lucky have tasted it," Mr. Yin says.

"Why?" Donald Duk asks, "Just because you know Dad wines and dines opera people?"

"These are hard times for the opera people. The Cantonese opera was banned, you know, during the Cultural Revolution. And the opera people *left* Canton, *left* China. That was almost twenty years ago. No more Canton for Cantonese opera. Only a few Cantonese like your father keep it alive. And we're thanking him by all of us coming here to put on this opera for your father, free. We all pay our own way. And the Sifu Donald Duk turned down big money to perform here for your father."

"He's doing this for my father? Why?"

"Oh, don't you know? You're twelve years old this New Year."

"So, what's so special about twelve years old?"

"There's one animal for every year. And there are twelve animals in the cycle. You are once around the twelve years. You're not a kid anymore."

"You mean I'm supposed to go see this opera of Uncle Donald Duk's? Oh, wow! I hate this Chinese New Year stuff more and more."

"Don't whine out in the street like that. And don't hunch over like that. You look too easy to rob," Mr. Yin says.

"I know how to walk. Dad taught me how to walk in Chinatown and not get beat up."

"Then why aren't you doing it?" Mr. Yin asks. "Look at yourself right now." Mr. Yin puts a hand on Donald Duk's shoulder and turns him toward the front window of a closed employment agency. The lights inside are out. Only a nightlight at the back burns. The front window is like a tarnished mirror. Over the dim white rows of three-by-five notecards advertising jobs for Chinese cooks in odd cities and states across the United States, Donald Duk sees himself.

He is slouching and hunched over. He looks like he's about to cry. Why? He knows how to walk. "How depressing," Donald Duk says at the sight of himself. Then, oh no! The Frog Twins are in the window! They are touching him, creeping all over him with their little froggy fingers.

"Oh, don't look so sad!" one Frog Twin says. "Ohh, such a long face!" the other says. "We have just the thing," one says. "Come with us! Quick!" the other says. "Oh, Mr. Yin, can I have your autograph?" one says. "Yes, come up. Come up! You can autograph our poster!"

Now they nudge and poke and tickle him in the ribs and pinch him. Now he is climbing the narrow stairs of an old Chinatown apartment building to the third floor to cram inside a small Chinatown room. Identical twin beds fill most of the room. Beyond the ends of the beds is barely space for a fold-up card table and two old folding chairs with cushioned seats. An electric hotplate and a microwave oven sit on the card table by the window. Across the window are strings. Vegetables hang from the strings, like socks, to dry in the afternoon sun.

"We are so happy you came by," one Frog Twin says. "We were hoping you would! Care for a cup of hot tea?" the other gushes. "Oh yes, have a cup of tea. It's no trouble. Now where is it?" one Frog Twin says and climbs on her bed and looks through shopping bags piled on a shelf. "We have something for you," the other says, looking under the bed. "Here it is!" one says, standing on the bed with a long narrow cardboard box in her arms. "Here it is!" the other says, standing up with one of the posters advertising Uncle Donald Duk's Cantonese opera.

"I thought you were looking for tea," Donald Duk says.

"Oh, that was merely a formality. But we do have tea. Like some?" the other Frog Twin says.

"Chuck Guillow's model airplane kit. The P-26A Peashooter. Twenty-one vacu-formed plastic parts," one says and hands the model plane kit to Donald Duk. "Will you please autograph this, Ah-Yin Sifu ahhh?" the other says. Both look identically so happy, Donald Duk has no idea why, and looks round the room for a reason.

"Oh, you too, Ah-Mr. Larry Louie!" both twins trill and chirp.

"Oh, no. I'm just a friend seeing you ladies safely to your door," the Chinese Fred Astaire says.

Now Donald Duk can go to the banquet and not be afraid. He can show Dad Chuck Guillow's model airplane kit and say he planned to burn and rebuild the P-26A all along. "Thank you," Donald Duk says. "It's just what I've always wanted."

"Oh, it's nothing," one says. "Nothing at all," says the other.

"Oh, no! It's Lee Kuey, the Black Tornado!" Donald Duk says.

He grins and holds the kit close to him. The looks on the Frog Twins' faces tell him they do not know what he's talking about. He doesn't know either. Lee Kuey is the name of the dark Chinese who grits his teeth and holds a battle-axe in each hand. He was painted on the model of the P-26A. That's all Donald Duk knows. The darks of one Frog Twin's eyes grow large and her grin grows big and sincere. She nods understanding. The other raises her eyebrows and the darks of her eyes grow large, and she grins and nods understanding. The sisters nod at each other and chuckle a croaky understanding laughter. They agree, they understand. They nod at Donald Duk. He does not know what they understand, even as he nods back and smiles back, and raises his eyebrows up and down. Why are the Frog Twins so nice to Donald Duk? Why do they give him just what he needs, just when he needs it? Do they know something he doesn't know? Do they know they have saved him from a stressful time worse than death? The sullen mood, the fear of bumping into his father, dodging him all day is gone because of this box of soft tissue paper, wire and balsa wood with twenty-one vacu-formed plastic parts. Donald does not ask what they know. He does not tell them what he knows. He says, "Thank you," and means it, and asks the way to the bathroom.

The hallways look longer than anyone expects from seeing the whole building between other buildings on the street. From one end of the building to the other, just walking by outside, is only a few steps. Inside, the building seems endless for all the little narrow doors on either side of the hall. The bathroom is at the end of the hall. The quiet in the hall rumbles with the voices of all the little TVs inside the little rooms turned low. Out of one room comes what sounds like Julio Iglesias singing "To All the Girls I Loved" in Cantonese. On his way down a strange musty hall past the doors closed to a thousand threats, screeching tires, wild gunshots, raging cars, burning trees, Donald Duk does not want any of the doors to open, any strangers from some strange insides to step out before he makes it to the bathroom and closes the door. Whoops! Just after he has a foot up and before he puts it down to finish a step, a door opens and his view of the white porcelain toilet with a black horseshoe-shaped toilet seat is blocked by a black and green camouflage pattern on a field jacket. "Are you following me, Donald Duk?" American Cong asks.

"I'm going to the bathroom."

"Why?"

"I have to pee."

"You mean, if I scared you right now, you would wet your pants?" American Cong grins, and his eyes shine hard and crazy into Donald Duk's. "I pissed my pants, Donald Duk. I thought all the yellow people of Asia ate rice. And here I am in a cornfield. A Montagnard cornfield. A perfect cornfield. Wow! Hey."

"Will you excuse me, please?"

"You didn't tell anyone about me, did you?"

"No."

"If anyone asks about me, tell them something for me: *Leave me alone!* End of message. Go pee." He turns up his collar and heads up the hall to the stairs to the roof.

"Oh, that's Ah-Jik's boy," the first Frog Twin says back in the room. "He's all right," the other says. "He is strange, though," one says. "But he's hardly ever around," the other says. "He only comes by to see his old auntie," one says. "He's a good boy," the other says. "Strange, though," one says.

"Strange," Donald Duk says with his kit under his arm.

9

WHOA! Dad's restaurant is full of a monster's immediate family loitering about the round tables like the waters of a marsh dawdling around knobs of high ground. They all have very dark piercing all-seeing eyes like Donald Duk's father's eyes.

One sunny day at the zoo Donald Duk sees eyes like his dad's in the head of a red-tailed hawk in a cage. The hawk looks pissed, wanting a fight, like his dad. He has never seen Dad's hawkeyes in the heads of so many Chinese before. They all seem to have five heads and ten arms. And there's five of everybody. Five grand Ah-Goong Goong Goong Goong Goong, five grandmas Ah-Paw Ah-Paw Ah-Paw Ah-Paw Ah-Paw. Five first sons and five first-son's wives and twenty-five grandchildren. Five second daughters and five second-daughter's husbands and twenty-five grandchildren. Five and twenty-five times five the same scenes of the life of the same Chinese family ripple through the people putting their backs to the world and closing up around their table. The spaces between the tables seethe a mass of children on the loose.

Big kids, little kids. Girls and boys. They rove in clumps of bobbing five-headedness. Five-headed babies bulging diapers crawl under the tables. Some five-headed people sit. Lots of five-headed hawkeyed people stand. Lots of five-headed people are caught up in the tide of milling children and torn away from their tables to clump up with other people, float on the roving children, sink in the quicksand of little hands waving to each other across islands of tables and rest against the shoals of straight-backed shiny-skinned old people who dye their hair charcoal black. The twins always elbow him in the ribs when they see dyed black hair on a head in Chinatown. Where is Arnold Azalea? A white boy should be easy to spot in this crowd of smoldering hawkeyes. Everyone acts like they live here. The kids look at Donald Duk like a stranger.

Larry Louie's face brightens up in the burbling noise. "It's like a gypsy caravan settling down for the night," the Chinese Fred Astaire says. He sucks at the noisy, buzzing air for a breath of sweaty people. He says, "This air is heady wine for the soul," and sighs.

"I was going to say it looks like a gang of Chinese outlaws plundering a mansion," gruffs Mr. Yin, the five-in-the-morning tai chi teacher and afternoon flamenco guitarist.

"You have your Spanish flamenco guitar in your hand while, inside this gaudy Chinese restaurant, you talk about Chinese outlaws. Don't you think that is a little strange?" Donald Duk asks.

"Gypsy caravan. Chinese outlaws. Same thing. Same theme. Robin Hood, Spanish gypsies, Jesse James all the same," the Chinese Fred Astaire says and giggles. What's funny about that? wonders Donald Duk.

And Mr. Yin chuckles and grunts as if what the Chinese Fred Astaire says makes sense. They don't seem to know that what they are saying sounds incredibly stupid. Or is Donald Duk stupid? Donald Duk does not ask this out loud. What kind of outlaws ride and raid with their families? Robin Hood does not run through Sherwood Forest with the old folks, wives and sweethearts and little babies. The James boys do not ride on Northfield, Minnesota, with the Youngers, camping out every night with their families.

Larry Louie and Mr. Yin don't know how stupid they sound. Here are Arnold Azalea's rich parents. Why is dad kissing up to Arnold's parents? Because they're white and rich?

"Your father is giving you face. He's showing you respect by treating your friend and his family as his own."

"That's stupid."

"That's the way Chinese fathers show you how important you are."

Dad is in the kitchen fixing up a family-style dinner his way. He's cooking without meat. The first dinner at home with the family on the first night of the first day of the new year is meatless. How meatless is meatless is a matter of family whim. Tonight. This year. The larger the immediate family, the less whimsical the meaning of meatless. Tonight: no meat, no animal fat. "Family-style tonight means the family lets me cook the stuff that no Chinese, no one on this earth has seen in a Chinese family dinner before. And yet, like Confucius himself, I will restore ways that have become abandoned and recover knowledge that has been lost," Dad yells as he splats tapwater on a bank of five hot woks. He doesn't turn down the squirt of flames ringing the bottom of every wok. The startled steel of the large woks clicks and sings. Dad's hands and arms disappear into the steam with bamboo brushes. He brushes the woks out with the heavy bristled brushes, wipes them out with clean new kitchen towels and seasons each of them fresh for the rest of the year with oil, garlic, ginger, black beans, sugar and sherry. The steam and smoke bloom and mushroom-cloud about Donald Duk's father as he tosses piles of raw shrimp paste and bowls of cold sliced fish and fruit, and waves his tools into and out of the roiling atmospheres.

"Oh, Godzilla versus the nuclear missiles," Larry Louie says and touches Donald Duk and Mr. Yin lightly on the arm as he stops. "I love it. I just want to be decadent and impolite and watch. Just for a sec, young man. Oh, look! Between the counter and the woks, it's so like a dance as he races the hot steel and cold foodstuffs. I love it! If I could move like that, I would be a star right now," the Chinese Fred Astaire says. Between moves Dad grabs looks at the little TV-set on a shelf of the steam table, tuned to the news.

Now Dad cooks up meatless originals mixing the common items of many cuisines into things wonderful, strange and tasty. Fettucini Alfredo with shark's fin. Poached fish in sauces made with fruit and vegetables. Olives on toast that taste like rare thousand-dollar caviar. Chocolate, bananas, yellow chili peppers, red chili oil and coconut milk go into one sauce over shredded chicken and crabmeat to be eaten rolled up in hot rice-paper pancakes with shredded lettuce, green onions and a dab of plum sauce.

The twins and Arnold Azalea pass each other around the steam table and chopping blocks, blenders, beaters and bins, going for this spice, that vegetable out of cold storage in a warm rhythm, as if everyone in the kitchen is a player in a well-tuned orchestra and Dad is the conductor, moving in and out of the steam of his woks, finishing and starting one dish after another.

Mr. Yin calls to Uncle Donald Duk splashing and sizzling at a wok all his own. The words lob out of his mouth like military commands. "Ah-Sifu!" (Maestro in Cantonese to Donald's Dad.) "Ah-King sook ahhh! Aha! Ah-Sook!" (Familiar but very respectful.) "*Ho see fot choy.* What an honor it is for me to see you working at your art!"

"Oh, Mr. Yin, you are too kind. You must be drunk and bleary-eyed. Take a look at your Sifu! He's the maestro here!"

"What are you Making, Ah-Sifu?"

"Dragon and Phoenix soup."

"Mr. Yin, please, find a seat outside and make yourselves comfortable," Dad says.

Mom suddenly appears, rushing toward Donald with her hands behind her back untying her apron. "Oh, Donald," she calls, "you better *bai sun* before you eat."

What? Donald asks. She hustles him through the swinging doors out of the kitchen into the dining room to an altar table where the flower arrangement is replaced with a family shrine. Before family emblems and photographs stands an incense burner with smoldering sticks of incense punk. A steamed chicken on a platter and three little rice bowls filled with perfect mounds of rice and three little teacups filled with tea, and a mound of tangerines and a perfectly shaped pomolo grapefruit with stem and leaves are all arranged in front of the incense burner. There is a little teapot with tea, should the ancestors care for more tea. There are little chopsticks to eat the rice with. There are little red envelopes arranged around the dishes. There is a bottle of Johnny Walker Red with the seal cracked open. The red envelopes of *lay see* are the donations of the immediate family to immediate family causes, the rainy-day fund, the war chest.

Mr. Yin takes a red envelope out of his pocket and slips it between other red envelopes. They ripple and fold like the scales of a fish, like the feathers of a hawk's wing. He burns yellow paper printed to fold into a fake gold ingot. No one bothers to fold paper. He kowtows three times with the burning paper gold, then drops it into a bowl of ashes just before the flames reach his fingertips. He lights a stick of incense and holds it in his right hand and covers his right hand with his left, like a swordsman in a kung fu movie meeting a swordsman on the road of life. He bows three times and gazes at the portraits of all the family dead a moment, then bows three times again, then looks at the photos again, then bows three more times. Nine bows in all, and adds his stick of incense punk to the others in the burner.

The children get down on their hands and knees and kowtow, bonking their foreheads on the floor three times and bowing three times. Donald Duk can't stand the thought of doing such a thing. He can't remember ever doing it. He feels more American for not doing it. He is shocked to see Larry Louie the Chinese Fred Astaire get down on his hands and knees and kowtow like a kid before pouring a little shot of Scotch for the dead. It's not right. The Chinese Fred Astaire should behave American, or why bother billing yourself as the Chinese Fred Astaire, Donald Duk smolders. Donald Duk should be the Chinese Fred Astaire, not this fake.

Mom does not ask Donald to do anything in front of the shrine but fishes out a package she's hidden under the table. "What's this Mom?"

"It's a kit for making a model p-26a Peashooter. Now you can go in the kitchen and tell your father what you did last night, before your father tells you. Show him you're ready to make it right by building this kit, see? You want to start the new year off on the right foot."

"I already have a kit, Mom. See, here? Chuck Guillow's."

"If you want to make two kits, I'm sure that will be fine, but I don't think you can build two kits in two weeks, son. Do yourself a favor. Just build one. Leave one of those boxes with me and go in to your father's kitchen."

"You're not coming in with me, Mom?"

"No, son. I should mingle with our guests."

The kitchen is steamier than ever. All the smells of cooking are multiplied five times as Dad cooks for three hundred people sitting at thirty banquet tables. No waiters tonight. It's a family dinner. The children serve. Children from each table are in the kitchen, picking up their portion of each course. First is Uncle Donald Duk's Dragon and Phoenix soup. "It's not really dragon and phoenix is it, Uncle Donald Duk?"

"No, the dragon is the shark's fin and the lobster in the broth. The phoenix is the broth made of chicken, duck, squab, guinea hen and bird's nest," Uncle Donald says and leaves the kitchen with his soup. Arnold is gone to serve his parents' table. The twins are gone to serve Mom's table. Suddenly the kitchen is quiet, all the voices of the children gone. He thinks it is going to be difficult talking to Dad through the shouting of the children, and it is very difficult now with nothing but the hissing of the woks and the splashing of the water.

Dad uncovers a wok. Dad's hawkeyes flash through the rising

mounds of steam. He looks like a hawk above the clouds, a cosmic chef playing the music out of live food and dried food. No meat. No wild birds. Donald loves the taste of the wild duck and Canada goose Dad roasts for Arnold Azalea's dad when he comes back from hunting, but sees no wild birds tonight.

"Dad, you may have noticed that the P-26A Peashooter model you made is missing from the ceiling," Donald Duk says. The rhythm of sizzling and hissing, tossing and clanging on the iron woks continues unbroken. "Dad, I took the plane down. And I took it up on the roof and lit the fuses you had on it, and I flew it down Grant and watched it blow up."

Dad is still the hawk about the clouds, flying on the spoon and spatula he waves in his hands. "You know today nobody is prepared to play the greatest part of the greatest character in the opera," Dad says. "I mean Kwan Kung. You play Kwan Kung, you are supposed to eat nothing but vegetables, rice and water and clean yourself out the day before you take the stage as the god of fighters, blighters and writers. You are playing the most powerful character in the opera.

"You are not supposed to look anyone in the face the day before and on stage unless you want to kill that character, because one look into your Kwan Kung eyes and he's dead. No sex. No meat. No talk. No company. You do everything alone. No one does anything for you. You cook what you eat. You are from the day before you start putting on the makeup . . . Kwan Kung. That's it. No other part in the opera makes you do anything like that. There are stories about the actor who played Kwan Kung recently and did not take the part seriously, and maybe slept with his girlfriend that night before he takes the stage wearing the red face and two-foot-long beard of Kwan Kung, and when he takes the stage his girlfriend's hair turns white and she has a miscarriage. She didn't know she was three months pregnant. Uncle Donald Duk tells me that because of stories like that—about opera stars everybody in the opera world knows, so they can check out the story for themselves to see if it's the real or the fake—nobody wants to play Kwan

Kung. Too risky. What if they accidentally forget and eat a hot-dog? Or one bite of a *cha siu bow* goes down their throat before they remember? Kwan Kung does not accept the mess-up of re-sponsibility allowed by Western psychology. Real men, real ac-tors, real soldiers of the art don't lose control. Just like Yin the Tat-tooed Wrestler in *The Water Margin,* when the most beautiful woman in the empire, Lee Shi Shi, coos and croons all her seduc-tive know-how on Yin, he never gives in and never forgets his mis-sion. Never.

"When I play Kwan Kung I eat nothing but vegetables three days before the performance. The last rehearsal two days before the performance is the last I see of the cast or anybody. I have a room. The day and night before the performance is off to rest our voices and meditate on the part we're playing, free association like with the part." The noises Dad strikes off the woks and the steel tools clang and gong a natural opera accompaniment to Dad's strange fit of talkativeness. Donald Duk wishes Larry Louie were here to listen. He would love it. Listening to Dad alone, what Donald hears doesn't sound all good.

"I stay in my room alone. No radio. No TV. No books. I bring my water in a bottle. I bring my own food. I soak dried oysters, dried vegetables, dried seeds and fruit and bean threads to make Monk's delight. The water restoring the dried things and the cooking of the restored mummied things makes up all the five ele-ments and the mandate of heaven. On stage Kwan Kung does not speak. I do not look anyone in the eye. I do not acknowledge the presence of anyone around me, unless I want them to die. I do not look the audience in the eye, unless I want them to die. I look over their heads to the back wall. They say when you play Kwan Kung, you are Kwan Kung. You enter with your eyes lowered. The in-stant you step on the stage, all magic and other bullshit disappears. Flying carpets don't fly. Ghosts are gone with their disguises. It's a great part, boy! It is a great part to play. All power. All presence. All dangerous. Hard to play. If you don't get it right, the part gets you, out there on the stage, and makes you pay, because Kwan Kung is always played right, or not at all.

"The greatest Kwan Kung I have ever seen onstage is your Uncle Donald Duk, my teacher. I take the part of Kwan Kung very seriously. I learned from the best. I eat no meat. Have no sex. No friends. No talk. No booze. No nothing before the performance, and I never think any disaster can ever come to be because I take Kwan Kung very seriously when I play him. Then my nice little baby boy turns out to be you."

Donald Duk is whapped dizzy. There's no one else in the kitchen to tell Dad that that is a terrible thing to say to his own twelve-year-old son. Donald Duk isn't twelve exactly. He has a few months of eleven left to live. How can Dad talk like this on the first night of the first day of the first month of the new year? Isn't this bad luck or something? Donald Duk can think of nothing to say. It seems too late to say anything when the swinging doors swing open with the sound of flapping pressure change between the steaming flaming kitchen and the air-conditioned hubbub in the dining room. The children clatter and clumpity-clump in for the next course to take back to their tables.

"Whoo! It's like a scene from *Planet of the Apes* out there," Venus trills. "No, I know the one you're thinking of," Penelope says.

"The one with Don Murray and the blond pretty guy with the teeth," Venus says. "Yes, James Franciscus," Penny says. "That's right," Venus yodels. "That wasn't *Planet of the Apes?*" The twins almost blur into one before Donald Duk's eyes and in Donald Duk's ears.

"No, I think it was *Conquest of the Planet of the Apes,*" Donald Duk says with something to say at last. The twins go back to the chopping blocks and sinks, and here comes Mom too, back to work shelling shrimp, busting crab, blanching chickens for Dad to finish and sauce in the woks.

"That's right!" Venus sings. "Our little brother is such a genius," Penelope sighs.

Donald shouts over the noise, "Dad! I got these kits! I can make a model P-26A just like the one you had, to take its place, okay?"

Dad swoops out of the steam to serve up thirty dishes for thirty tables. The children screech in and twitter like a hundred birds, grab the hot platters and are gone from the kitchen again. The longer he does not answer, the more Donald Duk feels his Dad means okay. "*Way!* Ah-King ahhh! Your only son wants to know if it is okay or not," Mom says with a little squawk in her voice.

Donald Duk is not close enough to the little TV to make out the face. It's Chinese. It looks like American Cong. The field jacket. The short hair. The bulky throbbing muscles. In custody. Body of a reputed Chinatown gangster killed early on the morning of the first day of Chinese New Year. Donald Duk can't listen to Dad and the TV too.

"If he wants to make a model airplane, he doesn't have to ask me. If he wants to replace the plane he stole, I don't okay talk. Only action." Dad says and splashes cold water on the hot woks and whisks out the steam with his new brushes, readying his iron for the next course.

Mom sets the dishes of ingredients for the next complicated course and whispers in tune with the spattering and whooshing water turning to steam and the clang of the water droplets dancing across the round sides of the wok. "Take that to mean okay, and get out to Uncle Donald Duk's table and start eating. You must be starved," she says like the voice of steam roaring out of Dad's woks. And Donald leaves the kitchen without a word.

Donald Duk will have to wait for the morning paper to know for sure, for sure he is the only one who knows the American Cong is orange, on Donald Duk's roof the night and time after midnight the Chinatown gangster is killed. Or he can watch the late-night news replays, see the pictures again, see the face and perhaps learn American Cong's real name.

10

THE NINE COURSES of the banquet come and go. The soup from
the land and sea. The long-dried-up food restored, the fresh food
slightly pickled. The opera people come and go. The night is over.
The restaurant is empty. The family dinner of the first night gur-
gles in the guts of hundreds now. Nothing happens. Nothing's
said. Arnold Azalea is happy and tired and anxious to rise for the
five-in-the-morning tai chi class with Mr. Yin at the White Crane
Club. Arnold falls asleep without a word. The lights are out in the
house. Now and then a firecracker explodes and echoes up and
down the street. Tomorrow the streets will be full of the smoke of
firecrackers, and Arnold will be able to hear and see Chinatown
gushing smoke from the tops of San Francisco's hills and tall
buildings. There are nothing but shadows over Chinatown, shadows on the misting night.

Dad likes the latest in big-screen color TV. Donald Duk keeps
the sound down low. He doesn't have to. Everyone in the family
watches TV whenever they feel like it. People in the bedrooms
down the hall can't hear it. To be sure no one hears and comes to
see what he's watching and asks him questions, Donald keeps the
stereo sound turned low and sits close to the big picture.

Homer Lee, ex-Marine, Vietnam vet. A murder suspect. Chinatown gang-related death of Fisheyes Koo, last seen alive leaving a Richmond District bar at closing time. Koo found dead near his car at the corner of Union and Kearney streets on Telegraph Hill. Lee fits the description offered by eyewitnesses of the murder. In custody. No alibi.

The cars cruising out of the Broadway Tunnel sound like a high wind pawing through the tops of tall trees hundreds of miles away from Chinatown. Up in the mountains, where Dad will never look for him, where the wind sounds like rubber tires rolling on asphalt, Donald Duk hears the voice of Fred Astaire, so casual, so friendly, so charming, "Donald, you'd better wake up before Kwan wakes you up."

"What did you say, Fred?"

"Don't forget your hat. It's going to rain."

Donald Duk opens his eyes and discovers no Fred Astaire there. He is dressed in a Chinese jacket like Uncle Donald Duk gave him, but more worn, black jeans, black workboots. "What's going on?" Donald Duk asks.

"Today we go for the world's tracklaying record, kid! Get the wax out of your ears!" and Donald is caught in the crowd of Chinamen drifting toward the *deem sum* people's camp in the dark blue of morning an hour or more before first light. The fires are lit already. The *juk* is made, hot and fresh. For a penny he gets a steaming bowl of fresh white *juk* and a dish of three steamed pastries stuffed with fish and chicken. Now that he is past asking her for *juk* and pastries, and past paying, he wants to stay and look at her.

Now Donald Duk is at the railhead in the light before dawn, standing in a drizzle with the shifters with their six-foot-long prybars, the hammermen with their nine-pound hammers, the tampers. Four hundred Chinese stand by the crossties, the gravel roadbed, all looking to Kwan the foreman, who waits in the rain for Crocker's go-signal.

Crocker is one of the Central Pacific's Big Four. Along with

Collis P. Huntington, Leland Stanford and Mark Hopkins, Crocker owns the railroad the Chinese are building. He is dressed in white. All white. White kidney-shaped riding britches, a white buffalo-skin jacket, a white pith helmet, white leather gloves and white riding crop for his white horse.

Under the patter and low of sunshine and rainclouds caught in the canvas of his tent, and the shadows of the rain running off the roof, Central Pacific Chief Engineer Strobridge clears his throat and plays for time with the reporters in his tent. "Uhhh. Er. Gentlemen, as you know, in the rush to make distance, the Union Pacific Railroad's Casement brothers have laid, in one day, seven miles and eighteen hundred feet on the Union Pacific end, a feat which Mr. T. C. Durant, vice president of the Union Pacific, wagers $10,000 cannot be beaten. I said to Mr. Crocker, 'We can beat them but it will cost something.' Mr. Crocker said, 'Go ahead and do it!' and this is how we will do it.

"The two lines are only twenty-five miles apart. We are within a few days of driving the last spike at Promontory Point, joining the Central Pacific and Union Pacific railroads into one transcontinental line. If I can beat the Casement brothers here, they will have no room to come back, even if they wanted. I have fourteen trains with five thousand men at my command as well as plenty of iron, ties, spikes, fishplates and material. Everything is ready and just in time. Just yesterday, the 27th, I picked my men, arranged my plans and got them properly placed to start at the foot of Promontory Mountain. I have two miles of rail loaded on a train with a double header to push it up ahead of the engines. So arranged, it can be unloaded close to the end of the last rail laid in the track, see.

"Well, this morning before sunrise, the whistle blew right on time. The two engines gave a lurch, the push bar broke and we are laid up, for now. But when the work does start, you will discern several gangs of men. One gang prepares and dresses the roadbed, shaping the riprap to receive the crossties, then another gang tamps the roadbed around the ties, while other gangs run the

crossties from where the wagons have dumped them to new roadbed and so on . . ."

Donald Duk stands with a hammer. He is short and small in a
gang of large Chinese. Kwan the foreman pulls Donald Duk out
of the gang and takes him to the head end of the track to Yin the
Wrestler.

"Kid, I need you here to dance in the lion, understand?" Kwan
claps a hand on Yin the Wrestler's shoulder and says, "Sifu, I'm
taking your oldest boy to drive spike." Donald Duk hands his
hammer over to Yin's first son.

Chief Engineer and Central Pacific Superintendent Strobridge
looks over the ready gangs through binoculars. "A gang will run
twenty-foot-long rails from the flatcars to the end of the track
where the crossties and roadbed are ready for them. More Chinese
will tool the rail into an exact position, gauge them and hold the
rail in place while others spike them down." Strobridge swallows
and stops to look over a well-dressed man's shoulder to grab a look
at the man's sketch of the lion dancers waiting for the beat and
firecrackers. "I admire that," Strobridge says. "I admire that
greatly." Then, "And behind the spikers another gang links the
rails with fishplates and wrenches the nuts and bolts tight." The
Chinese wear all black. Eight Irishmen with tongs stand on each
side of a forty-foot flatcar ready to unload forty-foot lengths of rail.
Now they all wait in the rain. The rain batters the crown and brims
of the Chinamen's hats till the brims sag and crowns ooze wet back
up through the felt. The rain splats on the hands holding sledge-
hammers.

The rain pops deep holes in the ground and splashes mud up the
white skirts and petticoats of society ladies from Sacramento and
Salt Lake City on a party car parked at the siding at the base camp,
where fourteen trains are all steamed up, oiled and ready to roll
with flatcars of rail to the end of track, and pull out the empties.
Well-heeled dapper railroad moguls with their families on show,
newspaper reporters from Salt Lake, St. Louis, *Harper's Weekly*

and Frank Leslie's *Illustrated Newspaper* and bigwigs of all kinds maul and kick up the mud, crowd their carriages, surreys, wagons, deck chairs, beach umbrellas and tables of catered munchies and liveried servants for a comfortable vantage under pavilions and large tents. The rain is too thick to see through to the railroad. People as close as the other side of the table disappear in the drench. The rain explodes makeup on the face, ruins ladies' eyes and turns light summer clothes transparent on the body, revealing the riveted and stitched structures of their underwear.

Crocker has muddy trouserlegs. His white horse is splashed with mud. Crocker prances his horse from camp to camp, making small talk and apologizing for the weather.

Kwan the foreman stands at the railhead, watching for Crocker's signal, and cusses loudly. A few of the well-dressed observers move their camps and chairs within twenty-five yards of the railhead to watch the Chinese waiting to start.

Kwan watches Crocker hold his muddy horse in place just in front of a pen-and-ink artist sitting under an awning. Kwan walks over to Crocker. He has to shout to be heard above the thud and plop, dribble, splash and tink of the rain bamming down down down. "*Way!* Hey! Ah-Crocker!" Kwan shouts. "We lose two hours, you *sahbay?* One mile track. Maybe two or three mile we lose already. You wanna we break that record or no?"

"Just hold on, Kwan."

"We start now or forget it for today."

"I want our guests to be comfortable when I make the new record."

"You make the record?" Kwan shouts. Kwan grabs the hammer out of Yin's son's hands and throws it up to Crocker on horseback. "You better be use some of that to break the record, don't you think?" Kwan turns to the gangs and shouts, "*Fong goong laaa!* Drop your tools!" The call is picked up and repeated down the line.

"If you leave now, you're fired, Kwan!" Crocker says and turns his horse to face the foreman.

"We are fired!" Kwan calls in a big voice to the Chinese gangs. "We are fired! Break camp! Pack it up! Break camp!" Kwan walks off shouting, "Break camp! We are fired!"

Crocker is embarrassed. He doesn't know what to do on horseback. He looks after Kwan and waits for him to turn, but Kwan does not turn and does not stop. He keeps walking away. Crocker turns to the little drenched encampment of the rich, young and powerful of Sacramento and Salt Lake City.

"Drop your tools! Break camp! We're leaving!" Kwan shouts along the line as he walks.

"What now?" Donald Duk asks out loud.

"It looks like we're leaving," the next man in line says. "You heard the man. Drop your tools." He drops his hammer and walks. The locomotive engineer leans out of his cabin and watches for the signal to start. He watches the gangs pass his wet and steaming engine.

Donald Duk catches up with Kwan just as Crocker gallops up and pulls up short by Kwan. The muddy white horse kicks mud up on Kwan and the gangs. Crocker walks his horse alongside Kwan and says, "Kwan, I spoke too sharply. I apologize."

"Get down off that horse if you want to talk to me," Kwan says, "or you get me a horse to sit on."

"I need you to win that $10,000 prize."

Kwan walks on. Crocker stops his horse and dismounts. He follows after Kwan on foot. "Kwan . . ."

"You want us to break the record, you get out there and pick up our tools. Be sure you put 'em away dry someplace. The first dawn the rain lets up, we break the record."

"I own the railroad, Kwan. You can't order me . . ."

"I build a railroad, Ah-Mist. Crocker. You do no own nutting me."

"Kwan, you are being recalcitrant and without reason," Crocker's words jiggle as his white horse is shy of Kwan.

"If our tools are dry tomorrow, we work. If not, we don't work,"

Kwan says. Kwan puts a hand on Donald Duk's back and shoves him forward as he begins to walk. Crocker hangs back, then catches up to Kwan.

"Kwan, I have always felt the deepest respect for you . . . your . . ."

"Let me ride your horse. I want to shoot your gun," Kwan says.

"What?"

Kwan has Crocker's sixgun in his hand, and before Crocker can drop his jaw in awe, Kwan is in the saddle with the reins in his hand. He wheels the horse this way and that, splashing mud all over Crocker. Kwan turns to Donald Duk, "Come on, kid. I want you to hear this . . ." Kwan lifts Donald Duk into the saddle behind him and rides off to the Chinamen's camp. Crocker chases after on foot, a white suit in a crowd of black. Kwan spatters a gallop into the *deem sum* people's camp and fires Crocker's sixgun three times. Donald Duk hangs onto Kwan by the waist and feels himself slipping off the back of the slippery muddy horse. "Tomorrow! Ten miles!" Kwan shouts. "Ten miles of track!" Looking across the wet desert, the pavilions of the bigshots are shadows. The clouds lay shadows slipping over their ground. Donald sees men, the glint of opera glasses and spy glasses aimed his way, when the sun lays bright over the edge of cloud and shadow.

Kwan turns the horse once around the area to look everyone in the eye. "They say it is impossible to lay ten miles of track in one day. We begin work at dawn. By sunset we will look back on more than ten miles of track. Do that and Crocker's horse here is ours to eat!"

Kwan rears the horse up and Donald Duk slips off and lands on his butt in the mud. The gangs, the *deem sum* people, all laugh and clap their hands. Donald Duk can't believe this Kwan is real. It's the eyes. They're like Dad's eyes, but more so. Where has he seen those eyes before? "Tomorrow! Dawn to sunset. Ten miles!"

Donald Duk looks around and sees into the door open into Yin's Kung fu family's wagon. Yin the Wrestler is costumed as

Kwan Kung and strikes a pose with Kwan Kung's Black Dragon Blade. Kwan Kung! This is the character in the opera who has the eyes that kill. This is the character everyone is chicken to play because they want to drink and gamble, smoke the waterpipe against doctor's orders and mess with women young enough to be their daughters, their granddaughters.

Donald is awake. His room. He listens to hear if he cried out or screamed himself awake. Arnold Azalea sleeps. No floorboards creak. No doors swing on their hinges anywhere in the house. Okay. His heart is not too fast, not too loud, not pounding at a valve in a vessel up the side of his neck.

Donald Duk pads along the hall carpet with expert silence to look at a wooden statue on the mantle—Kwan Kung, robed on his left side like a scholar. His right side shows exposed general's armor. His left hand holds an open book of Confucius. His right hand lifts his two-foot-long beard off his belly. He has the eyes of Kwan the foreman.

11

WITH A PUSH FROM INSIDE, Donald Duk is up at four-thirty and sleepy in the shadow of Russian Hill with Arnold Azalea, going to tai chi at the White Crane Club with Mr. Yin, doing tai chi very slowly with the dawn, then home as the sun rises for a shower and dressing up in a jacket and tie for the snooty private school, but first, breakfast with Dad and Mom and the twins at Uncle's Café on Clay Street, where the waffles are a legend half a century old. At school all the student body wears new *minop* jackets. Gifts from Uncle Donald Duk. Everything Uncle Donald Duk does, everything about this Chinese New Year is slathered in red and gold, gaudy, crude and obnoxious. Why can't the Chinese leave Donald Duk alone here at school, Donald Duk wants to know.

The sun sets early in late January and early February, when Chinese New Year falls. It's only four in the afternoon and already it's getting dark. There's Donald Duk in his jacket and tie standing with a Chinatown kid talking into his little walkie-talkie with the floppy antenna. The Chinatown kid wears a black tanker jacket, white tee shirt, dark glasses. Black hiking boots. A thin gold chain and a jade circle dangle around his neck. An old American car swings around the corner, hugs the inside lane and stops by Donald Duk. A Chinatown kid inside the car hands Donald Duk a shopping bag and drives off. Donald Duk nudges Arnold Azalea and they walk on without looking back. The windows of the shops are all lit up. Donald Duk notices all the figures and posters of Kwan Kung, the god of fighters, blighters and writers, lost among all the families of thermos bottles, trick guns in a variety of colors, plastic ivory tusks carved into arching pageants, real carved ivory tusks, teacups, horses, swords and petrified viscera. Kwan Kung the red-faced, fierce-eyed and bearded one in green. And the white-faced one in yellow holding a bag. And the black-faced, pop-eyed, whiskered one holding Kwan Kung's halberd. The three of them are in many kinds of posters, rendered by many artists. New posters, new renditions of the three seem to pop onto the Chinatown scene every now and then. Donald Duk suddenly remembers Kwan Kung posters of the three he does not see any longer. The three—the red-faced, the white-faced, the black-faced—are a set of statuettes and come in various sizes.

"How much did you get?" Arnold asks.

"All of it," Donald Duk answers.

"M-80s?"

"Two gross."

"Bottle rockets?"

"Yeah, everything."

Donald Duk glances into a butchershop window. On the back wall above the chopping blocks and bandsaws, Kwan Kung on horseback is painted on the textured wall. Next door Arnold Azalea admires a set of samurai swords in the window. Donald Duk's eyes catch on a wooden shrine on the back wall. Electric candles and plastic replicas of incense punk with little tiny electric red lights on the end glow in front of a glass painting of Kwan Kung and the white-faced one and the black-faced one. Real tangerines and leaves and stems are stacked on the shrine. Donald moves to the next window and looks in and sees, low on the floor of the

Chinese-Vietnamese soup palace, another wooden shrine. A little open porch, looking much like the rear platform of a caboose, or private railroad car. A door and a roof connected to each other by a back wall. The front is open. Along the sides are wooden fences running from the back wall to the posts at the front corners. Chinese fencework in wood looks like a brick wall with all the bricks disappeared and only the pattern of mortar left. All painted red.

The statue of Kwan Kung inside is gaudily painted wood. All primary colors. Kwan Kung's red face is red from the grade-school poster paint. His green robe and armor are greener than money, greener than the school lawn. This is the Kwan Kung the people living on boats in Hong Kong keep. Wood is lighter than porcelain. The punk is real.

The candles are electric. The pomolo grapefruit is real. The shrine on the floor looks like Kwan Kung in a boat. Is that why they keep their Kwan Kung on the floor here? Because these are boat people? Donald Duk lives all of his life at the same Chinatown address on Grant, walks by these shops every day, eats in most of the restaurants in the course of a year, yet doesn't remember seeing all the Kwan Kung statues and posters in the shrines everywhere.

"Have you seen all the shrines with the god of war all over Chinatown?" Arnold Azalea shouts above the muttering of Chinatown in rush hour gridlock.

"Pardon me, son, but can you tell me where I may buy firecrackers?" Donald Duk turns to see the pouches of a white man's face dangling low to speak into Donald's face, eye to eye. Donald Duk chokes and panics frozen. The white man takes it Donald Duk has trouble understanding English. Arnold Azalea steps into a curio shop doorway to watch the scene through the glass. "You speak English, son? Firecrackers?" the white man asks.

Donald Duk looks blank then shakes his head. He notices a white woman a few steps behind the white man looking very concerned, watching very closely. Police? He has a hundred dollars' worth of firecrackers, rockets, M-80s in his hand. "You know," the white man pleads slowly, carefully mouthing and shaping every syllable, "fire-crackers?"

Donald Duk shakes his head and points at his ears, then at his mouth, and shakes his head. He shoots a plaintive look at the white woman and points at his ears and mouth and shakes his head, shrugs his shoulders, holds his hands palms up, holding an imaginary bowl full of helplessness.

"You tell me where buy fie-err kerr-acker."

Donald Duk shakes his head. He points at his ear and shakes his head and shrugs. He points at his mouth and shrugs and shakes his head. The white woman creeps up on the white man and pulls on his sleeve by the elbow. "Jimmy, I think . . . I don't think he can hear you."

So the white man shouts, "FIE-ERR-KERR-ACKER! You know, son, shhh boom! God dammit!" he turns to her as she pulls at his sleeve again. "What?"

"Look at him, Jimmy. He can't hear. He can't speak."

Donald Duk shakes his head and mumbles blubbery sounds with a lot of gagging and lip. He points at his ears. He points at his mouth. The white man finally comprehends and jumps back, embarrassed. He takes out his wallet. "Oh, you poor kid!" he says softly and puts a five-dollar bill in Donald Duk's hand. "Here. I'm sorry, son . . . "

The white couple continues on up the street. Arnold Azalea passes by them as he catches up with Donald Duk. "Whew!" Donald Duk says.

Late that night, at a three-way intersection making a "Y" in a rich residential hilly San Francisco neighborhood, Donald Duk and Arnold Azalea set up an ambush. They set up a row of bottle rockets aimed at the center of the intersection. "A car coming down that hill into the intersection will present itself as a frontal target for our rockets, okay?" Donald Duk says. The boys hide behind the cement footing of an iron fence and wait for the prey.

"What if your dream is true, Donald?" Arnold Azalea says. "What if there really was a contest for the world's tracklaying record?"

"Ahhh! Even if it was real, the Chinese lost. They didn't do a thing but stand there and get soaked."

"Well, if the rain had stopped or that locomotive didn't go off the rail . . ."

"Ahhh! "

"I bet there was a contest like that."

"Headlights!" Donald Duk says.

The boys blow on their punks and ready themselves at the rocket fuses. Donald and Arnold are sweating already when they see the car and light the fuses. The fuses are still burning when the car is going away. The rockets take off, leaving a trail of sparks, and fall to the street. No hits.

The boys run out from their hiding place with an empty one-pound coffee can. Donald Duk puts an M-80 cherry bomb on the manhole cover in the center of the intersection, and the coffee can over the M-80. He runs a long fuse from the manhole cover to the hiding place behind the fence. They wait again. Donald sees the beams of headlights turning down the hill toward the intersection and lights the fuse to the M-80. Arnold lights the fuses to the bottle rockets.

"It's a police car!" Arnold Azalea says. The fuses are still burning when the black-and-white police cruiser rounds the corner and stops on top of the manhole cover, with its headlights shining into the boys' eyes. The rockets take off, leaving trails of pretty sparks.

The M-80 explodes, booming the coffee can to whang off the bottom of the police car. The explosion echoes mightily in the manhole to the sewers just as all the bottle rockets hit the windshield with little taps and thumps. The copcar doors swing open and two cops hop out behind the doors with their guns drawn.

Run! No one has to say it. The boys run to the back of the large front yard. Donald Duk climbs gingerly up on a wooden gate and looks over to see a policeman with a drawn gun creeping toward the gate. Donald drops down with a silence that amazes him and grabs Arnold Azalea and they run. One cop chases them on foot. The other screeches off in the car to chase the kids around the block.

Inside a San Francisco police station that looks like a Stop 'n' Shop without gas pumps, a hundred dollars' worth of explosive fireworks of all sizes lies on a steel table in a sterile room. Bouquets of bottle rockets. Mounds of M-80s. Stacks of packs of firecrackers. Arnold Azalea's parents, Donald Duk's parents, Donald and Arnold and the cops from the car are in the room. The cops scoop up the fireworks, put them in a garbage bag and take them out of the room. Dad shakes his head.

"We would understand perfectly if you would rather Arnold not spend two weeks in your house, King."

"But your trip, your second honeymoon," Mom says.

"Oh, we can take Arnold along. We've done it before."

"Oh, Arnold's a good boy. It's Donald!" Dad says.

"The boys have been planning this visit for so long, why ruin it and your honeymoon too? I mean, they are both good boys. They'll be fine," Mom says.

"Dad, you promised me," Arnold says.

"You two lovebirds go on to Hawaii," Mom trills. "The boys will be just fine. We are romantics ourselves. We love romance, don't we, King dear?"

"Sure, I just love romance."

"Of course, we'll leave Arnold with something to cover his legal expenses." Arnold's mother says.

"Oh, we won't hear of it, dear. Arnold is Donald's guest," Mom says so tra-la-la.

"Mom," Donald Duk whispers into her ear, "Mrs. Azalea was joking."

"Yes, wasn't that nice of her?" Mom answers happily.

Dad sends the boys and the twins to bed and doesn't want a lot of talk about it. "Dad," Venus says.

"Sleep!" Dad booms. Lights out. Dad turns the lights out in the bedrooms. The twins say goodnight. Donald and Arnold say goodnight. The hall light shows through under the door. Donald Duk does Bruce Lee and sneaks up in the shadows to the door and peeks out. Dad joins Uncle Donald Duk in the dinner room. Uncle Donald Duk works on his model plane. Dad sits behind the fuselage halves and wings pinned to the workboard and zaps the TV on with a remote control. Uncle Donald Duk pours a shot of Ng Gah Pay into a teacup and holds it out to Dad.

"Ng Gah Pay. The good stuff. From the mainland. I made it myself. Ha ha."

Dad takes the cup and sniffs the insides. He leans back and sings. He salutes Uncle Donald Duk with a tip of his cup, and just as he raises the cup to his lips, he hears thumps and laughter from Donald Duk's room.

Dad opens the door to the dark bedroom and looks at the boys faking sleep. "What's going on in here, girls? I don't know if I can leave you young ladies in the same room tonight. I don't know what's wrong you, Donald. I'm taking you to the herbalist tomorrow to see what we can do about you." Arnold squirts a little stifled laugh. "I'm glad to hear you're still friends. It's nice to have friends at New Year. It's good luck."

12

A LARGE GLASS BOTTLE holds a huge ginseng root about the size of a Cabbage Patch Doll and shaped like a man. A little blob of root is his head. He has arms and a bulbous body, legs and a little penis with hairlike roots dangling around it. The ginseng is ginger yellow with a pink blush at the joints between the bulbs. It floats in a jar of alcohol. On top of the bottle's flat stopper is a fine-looking little porcelain statue of Kwan Kung on horseback with his weapon. The insides of the shop look dark like a painting of something old. The bits of faces and hands and backs of heads Donald Duk sees seem emerging from very wet mud.

The herbalist is not from the funny papers. He does not wear a skullcap and bedroom slippers. The herbalist does not even look old or wear wire-frame glasses. He works behind the counter in his red Disneyland tee shirt. Behind him is a wall of wooden drawers. Each drawer a little smaller than a letter-size file cabinet drawer.

Each drawer holds a different dried flower, leaf, seed, stem, bark, root, tuber or berry of a medicinal plant. Scales, choppers, grinders of ivory, brass, steel and stone and a pile of prescriptions being filled are on the counter. He piles the ingredients of each prescription on the center of a clean square of butcher paper. The Chinatown Fiddler Donald Duk hears late at night sits in the herb shop window. Four or five old men are stringing their musical instruments around the shop.

Donald Duk steps into the shop with his father, King Duk. He can't take his eyes off of the Chinatown Fiddler, who's looking over the herbs and dried and variously preserved medicinal animals and animal parts displayed in the window around the big ginseng plant in a jar. The fiddler strings and tunes his double-stringed fiddle. His eyes move from seahorses to antler horn, one object to another, as if they are parts of a puzzle, as if they can combine to have a single meaning, a plot, a hidden message for the knowledgeable eye. He calls to the herbalist.

"*Wuhay!* Hey! Ah-Chuck! These seahorse good for sexy?"

"Old garlic fart like you better not even talk about seahorse without first being sure you have a woman. You don't want to waste the seahorse."

The old men and Dad break out laughing. "You listen to me, now!" the Chinatown Fiddler says, and the men laugh harder. Through a doorway there's a back room. More than one back room. Two old Chinese in suits and ties play Chinese chess with their hats on at a wooden table painted in green enamel. They don't laugh. The herb doctor has a shaved head. He wears a skullcap. He looks like something from the funny papers.

"All this stuff—deer antler, dried seal gonads, everything in the window—is good for sexy sexy. What if I took just a little of everything in the window in a little bowl of tea?" the Chinatown Fiddler asks.

"The thrill of all that wild animal power going bang in your body will kill you thirty seconds after your first swallow," the herb doctor says.

The herb doctor wears a sweater that buttons in the front. His back office is carpeted. Over the carpet are Chinese rugs. There is a couch. Easy chairs. He sits behind a large rosewood desk. He motions Dad into the easy chair at the front of the desk. "Tea," the herb doctor says. "A little silver needles. You can't get it in the restaurants in this city. You look to be healthy and prospering. I hear good good things about you. I see no fever about you. No ice in your eye. No winds howling in your bones. Your lungs are clear. Your breath doesn't come out cold. You are fit to fight a crazed ox, little brother. I know you're not here for your health then."

"It's my son."

"Ah! Certainly. Come sit here, boy," the herb doctor waves Donald Duk to sit in another easy chair at the front of the desk.

Donald Duk sees no doctor's tools, no shiny stainless steel instruments on the herb doctor's desk, and sits. "Here," the herb doctor says, "put your wrist on the pillow, here, boy." He guides Donald Duk's hand to lying back down, palm up on a little velvet pillow.

The herb doctor stands and washes his hands at a little sink in a little bathroom off his office. "How old are you?"

"Eleven. I'll be twelve this year."

"Skinny for eleven. What's the matter, boy? Don't your parents feed you at home?" The herb doctor laughs and lays his fingertips on Donald Duk's exposed wrist and reads the pulse. "Hmmm. What seems to be the problem, Ah-King Sook?"

"I feel fine," Donald Duk says.

"He's acting strange," Dad says. "He's jumpy and jittery, tapping his toes and clicking his heels all the time like someone with a palsy."

"Hmmm," the herb doctor says. "Your other hand, please, boy."

"And he steals from me and lies, and treats Chinese like dirt."

"I do not!"

"I think I may have accidentally taken home a white boy from the hospital and raised him as my own son. And my real son is somewhere unhappy in a huge mansion of some old-time San Francisco money."

"Stick out your tongue," the herb doctor says. Donald Duk sticks his tongue out. The herb doctor plays a flashlight on it and reads Donald Duk's tongue.

"I can't believe I have raised a little white racist. He doesn't think Chinatown is America. I will tell you one thing, young fella, Chinatown is America. Only in America can you run to any phone book, any town, look under C and L and W and find somebody to help you," Dad says. Donald Duk doesn't laugh. "He doesn't understand a Chinatown joke either," Dad says.

"Now stick out your tongue and lift it up as far as you can. More. More! Lift! Lift it up!" the herb doctor coaxes and growls as he plays the beam of a pocket flashlight over Donald Duk's tongue and reads it. "*Ho luh!* Good," the herb doctor says and snaps the flashlight off, pocketing it.

"Good," the herb doctor says again, smiling. He pours Donald Duk a cup of tea from a silver thermos on his desk, then shoves a dish of yellow raisins across his desk to Donald Duk. "These will freshen your mouth," he says. "It's no fun sticking your tongue out like that at me, I know. And your tongue gets dry." He glances at Dad as he speaks.

"Thank the herb doctor," Dad says low, slow and too friendly.

"Thank you," Donald Duk says. His tongue feels like a dry sponge stuffed in his mouth. He sips the tea and pops a couple of raisins in his mouth. His tongue is no longer Death Valley, and feels like a tongue again.

The herb doctor looks through his notebooks and makes notes. He looks from one notebook to the other to his new notes, then lowers his glasses to go eye to eye with Donald Duk. "Do you have a girlfriend?" he asks.

"No."

"Do you think about girls a lot?"

"No."

"Hmmmmm. Hmmmm." The herb doctor looks up from his notes again. "Do you think about boys the way boys think about girls?"

"No."

"Whew!" Dad says.

"Hmmm," the herb doctor says, then opens another notebook and glances from one open notebook to another, then writes in his notebook.

"You're not going to tell me this is just puberty are you?" Dad asks.

"Oh, no. This is more serious than that," the herb doctor says.

"Well, cousin, what is it?"

"I would say this boy has a bad case of gotta dance!"

"Gotta dance!" the Chinatown fiddler shouts in the front of the shop and his monkey squeaks. The other old men hum.

"Gotta dance! What's that?"

"Gotta dance can't be cured with herbs," the herb doctor says.

"Gotta daaaance!" Donald Duk sings and strikes a Fred Astaire pose, singing a Gene Kelly song.

"Gotta daaaance!" the old men in the front sing. Donald Duk dances out of the shop into a crowd, and Fred Astaire falls in step with Donald Duk.

"Who do they think they are? I'm smarter than any of them," Donald Duk says.

"You sure are," Fred Astaire agrees with a smile.

"I'm smarter than all of them put together."

"No argument there," Fred Astaire says.

"Well, I am!"

"You don't have to convince me."

"What do they know?"

"Compared to you?"

"Yes, compared to me. What do they know?"

"Oh, compared to you ... well ..."

"They know nothing! I know calculus, physics ..."

"That's a lot to know right there. Quite a lot indeed! Very good."

"They don't even know how to adjust the color on the TV."

"Shocking!"

"They make everybody on the TV look Chinese! Don't they know this is America?"

"Who could forget that?"

"Oh, you don't know these people like I do. Not only have I been living with them, I have been reading up on them. You know why after all the years they've been here, they're not more American?" Donald Duk asks.

"More American?"

"American! Like you and me. The kind of people who make American history. The kind of people actors play in American movies."

"Oh, yes, those kind of people."

"You know why the Chinese can't be that kind of people?"

"Why?"

"Passivity."

"That?"

"Not only that! They're not competitive. Can't stand the pressure."

"No!"

"They lost a tracklaying contest when they were building the railroad, just because they were too chicken to work in the rain."

"Didn't I read someplace that a locomotive derailed back at the terminal?"

"That too. But it was the rain."

"How slippery of them."

"They can't do anything right here."

"It's a wonder they manage at all."

"I'm not like them."

"Oh, no," Fred Astaire says. "That's obvious."

"I'm like you. You know what I'm talking about. We speak the same language. We talk the same lingo. We dig the same jive."

"Oh, we sure do."

"I'm better than that old broken-down Chinese Fred Astaire. I have real music. I have rhythm and music. I could be the Chinese Fred Astaire right now if I wanted to."

"Oh, easily. Easily."

"When I said I could be the Chinese Fred Astaire right now, I didn't mean I was really better than you."

"Oh, go ahead, say you mean it. Don't be shy," Fred Astaire says, the words riding a happy crooning chant. "For, oh my, a goodly number of years now, kids your age, a few kids your age have known they can dance Fred Astaire better than Fred Astaire. I'm flattered. And ask any of them. I am always happy to do anything I can to help. You do . . . want to dance Fred Astaire better than Fred Astaire, don't you?"

"No, just better than that pitifully poor imitation who calls himself The Chinese Fred Astaire. That's all."

"That's all you want," Fred Astaire looks bewildered. He puts his left hand in his trouser pocket and scratches behind his right ear with his right hand as if about to burst into dance.

Cold Jell-O air. The far mountains, the clumps of odd bushy plants popping out of the desert at strange angles, everything in the cold is like canned fruit cocktail in a blue gelatin dessert. A pale rumor of light outlines the dark of the far mountains from the dark of the night. The moon broods large on the horizon and is fiery red like a bite of raw meat, glowing through the dust of a recent volcano eruption. The flames of the woodfires burn in the fireplaces and stoves of the *deem sum* people ready to start serving. The Frog Twins wearing all the nineteenth-century clothing they own still look the same and fuss over a bun concession.

Kwan sees the first light over the far mountains and finishes his tea in one more swallow, puts his teacup down and has every eye in the *deem sum* people's camp on him. He puts a good-sized dark cigar in his mouth, lights it with an ember from a *deem sum* fire and walks to the edge of the railroad camp. A string of 10,000 firecrackers hangs from a rope attached to a pole. Boys and girls from the *deem sum* camp hold the rope and poles. A boy with a

gong and mallet waits by the string. Kwan lights the fuse to the
string of firecrackers with his cigar. The firecrackers begin cracking one and two at a time, then ratatatat, then a roar of continuous
overlapping explosions. The boy with the gong beats chang chang
chang changa changachanga on the gong through the railroad
camp. "Wake up! Wake up! Today! Today is the day! Ten miles.
Ten hours."

Donald Duk wakes up in a tent with other boys waking up to
the gusting and gushing firecrackers cracking, and the smell of
gunpowder blowing down the line of tents.

First light. Time to eat and tea before dawn. Donald Duk wears
a flat-brimmed black hat, a blue denim shirt with a Chinese collar
and cuffed sleeves, black denim jeans held up with a black leather
belt two inches wide, black boots. He buys a bun from the Frog
Twins, who give him an extra one for free. He munches his buns
and wanders through the crowd working themselves up to go to
work. He comes to Yin the Wrestler's Kung fu family's camp.
Where is Yin now? Still costumed as Kwan Kung? The girl about
Donald Duk's age works out with a spear next to the family's medicine wagon. Small children and the very old of the *deem sum*
people's camp watch her and mutter to each other with smiles on
their faces. The back of the wagon opens up. A wheelbarrow-like
cart to carry a drum rolls out backward behind Yin. On the cart is
what looks like a big whiskey barrel with some of the top and some
of the bottom cut off, and covered with a buffalo hide to make a
big loud drum. A young man takes up pulling the drum cart. Yin
the Wrestler beats the rhythm on the hide, on the edge of the
drumhead, on the steel rivets holding the skin to the sides.

Four other men carry a dancing lion. Its movable ears flop up
and down. Its movable eyes bounce partially closed and open. The
movable lower jaw wags a little. The white beard sways. Even un-
manned it looks alive. Drugged but alive. One carries the head.
One carries the tail. And two carry staves.

"Come on, boy! Today we make history!" Yin the Wrestler calls.

Yin and his Kung fu family wheelbarrow their big drum to the railhead, carrying their gongs and cymbals and the bamboo-and-papier-mâché lion head. Yin the Wrestler beats the drum. The family beats the brass. Chinese work along the way, meet the tool wagons. Some take bars and hammers off the moving wagon and walk on. Others climb onto the wagons and ride to the end of track.

The steel-tired, wooden-wheeled tool wagons stop along the gravel right of way where the work will begin. Horse-drawn wagons loaded with crossties are ready to roll.

In the chief engineer's tent, artists and reporters from the newspapers and magazines sit in camp chairs provided by the railroad and sketch by Chief Engineer and Superintendent J.H. Strobridge's lamplight. Strobridge is a tall, black-bearded man with the sad eyes of a spaniel. Along the line of tents and pavilions, Charles Crocker rides his white horse, wearing his white outfit and sporting his sidearm and riding crop.

Kwan stands at the head end, facing the gangs, waiting for the start. He bellows each word one whole at a time. His voice echoes in the murky light before dawn. "One day! The Irish lay four miles of track! Between sunrise and sunset! Four miles! World Record! We lay six miles! World Record!"

Donald Duk sees the politicians and railroad barons at the windows of their custom-built parlor cars straining to hear Kwan, and laughs. They don't undertand Cantonese. Donald Duk understands every word Kwan the foreman says. "One day! The Irish say, *We make ten miles in one day!* They get up! Start work at three in the morning! Dark! They work by lamplight! They work till midnight! Twenty one hours! How many miles? Ten miles? Did they lay ten miles of track? No! Nine miles? No! Eight miles? No! They lay seven miles and eighteen hundred feet! Seven miles, eighteen hundred feet in twenty-one hours is a joke! We make five miles in ten hours without working hard. We will not work twenty-one hours or eighteen hours and call it a day's work! We start work at sunrise. We stop work at sunset. Ten miles! Ten hours! Ten miles! One day's work!"

The gangs cheer. They shout, "Ten hours! Ten miles! One day's work! Ten hours! Ten miles! One day's work! Ten hours! Ten miles! One day's work!"

A white missionary in a clerical collar and a white buckskin jacket with swaying black fringe translates for Strobridge and the artists and writers under the awning of Strobridge's tent. He strains to hear the shouts precisely through the drips and dribblings of old rain and dew warming in the cold light. "Ten hours! Ten miles! One day's work!"

"That is one arrogant fellow, that what's-his-name Chinese," a writer quips afterwards.

"Kwan is his name. Kwan the foreman," Strobridge says.

"A Chinese foreman?"

"All the foremen are Chinese, gentlemen. Up in the Sierra Nevadas we encountered solid granite mountains. We had no choice other than blasting tunnels through with nitroglycerin, an impossibly temperamental new explosive no one but the Chinese dared play with. One terrible winter in the high mountains, followed by a worse winter in the higher mountains, and when you are once again comfortable in your work, confident the worst is over and the Chinamen are civilized, they go on strike. They would not work without their back pay being paid up and Chinese foreman for the Chinese gangs. The wisest thing the railroad ever did was to agree to the Chinamen's demands, for no sooner did they have their pay due them in their hands, then they asked for an increase in their pay. The railroad refused, with trepidation, I might add. But the Chinamen had made a deal and they kept it, though they knew it was short of what they might have gotten, had they asked first."

Kwan watches and sees dawn crack over the mountains and lights the fuse to a rocket. The gangs on the ground watch the rocket trail sparks and explode. Drivers whip up their horses.

Lumpers hang on. Wagons roll out. The head end gang tamps the riprap roadbed around the crossties. Eight Irishmen grab a forty-foot length of steel rail off the head end flatcar and sixteen Chinese nab it with tongs and trot it past the doubled locomotives to its place and trot back. The rails are grunted and nudged and gauged and lined by one gang chanting commands and calls that become a song. Another gang bolts the fishplates together and wrenches the nuts and bolts tight to hold one rail end to end with another for the continuous steel ribbon shining across the desert. Crossties. Tampers. Gaugers and pushers, spikers and nuts and bolts.

Just ahead of the head end gang Yin the Wrestler's Kung fu family beats the lion out of the hide drum and brass razzle dazzle. The older children dance the Cantonese lion. The girl twin Donald Duk's age teases the lion with her staff and dances in taunt and play with the lion. Her movements with the staff and her body are a puzzle to watch. Donald Duk stays close to the lion and is drawn to the sweet fighter with the staff. He can't dance. He can't lift rail or drive spike. He feels too small, and it's an odd feeling, for he sees all the Chinese. Even the biggest look hardly larger or older than him.

The work kicks up a lot of dust. A new section of rail is laid. Eighty feet. A brakeman at the new railhead passes a hand signal to the engine with his leather mitts to come ahead. The locomotive shudders and screeches inside as steam pressures change in chambers, condensers, tubes, valves and tanks inside and outside the iron-and-brass boiler. All the flatcars of steel rails thump and give out the sounds of snapping iron and creak strange shrill musical sounds as brakemen on each car fine-tune the chains that tie the brakes against the steel wheels. Just sitting alone on the flatcars, the steel rails sing and ping, stretching in the sun, warming up, getting hot. It sounds like dropping quarters into the punchbowl to Donald Duk, but spookier, more alive. The rails snap like knuckles, crackle like hot oil in the wok. The steel radiates the cold of last night and sounds like liquid, sounds like bone and chilled muscle.

The locomotives shove the flatcars gingerly, delicately to the conductor's hand signals, slower, slower, screaming inches to a stop just short of the end of the last rail spiked home to the ground. The brakemen tie the brakes on. The last screw turns off the brake wheel. They fulcrum with their axe handles to draw the chains tight enough to twang.

The politicians share a morning shot of booze while watching the panorama of steam locomotives, loaded and squealing railroad cars of gleaming steel and 400 Chinese visibly, perceptibly, obviously moving the railroad forward, eastward. As each flatcar of rail is stripped bare, twenty Chinese line up on one side of the rail and push and lift one side of the empty flatcar up off the track and tip it over and off the tracks. Before the dust settles, the conductor passes the hand signal to the locomotive to come ahead slow, and the next loaded car creaks up. When all the flatcars are wheels up on the ground, the locomotives deadhead back to the barn for another loaded train of rails.

A boy dances the head of the lion, his upper body is inside the head, his legs doing variations of kung fu moves are the lion's front legs. The boy's arms are the bones inside the lion's neck, lifting the head off his head, pushing the head out in front of him with his arms. The lion lunges and twists, lurches and arches. The ears and eyes move when the boy inside pulls the right string inside the head. The lion's lower jaw dangles open over the boy's chest and belly.

Now and then he uses one hand to flap the jaw up and down, or lifts the lion head up and works the jaw with his thumbs. The boy inside catches Donald Duk's eye and calls for relief. Donald Duk hesitates for an instant, but dancing is dancing, hey hey hey! The boy in the lion lifts the head off and pushes it into Donald Duk's hands. Donald Duk ducks under and inside the lion's head and grabs. The drums and gongs are muffled under the enormity of the sound of the work of iron on rock and steel on steel and 400 pairs of feet crunching gravel right of way. Donald Duk dances the lion and loses track of time till the locomotive gives out a long thirty-second blast of its steam whistle. The clatter and crash of hundreds of hammers striking hundreds of spikes subsides and stops. The last bit of their sound ripples away into the desert.

Donald Duk climbs out of the lion head. "Why are we stopping?"

Tourists and writers and Strobridge the Chief Engineer move along with the work in their buggies and wagons. Kwan the foreman's voice rises from the distant daylight silence in answer to Donald Duk's question. "Lunch! Luuuuunch! One hour! One hour for luuuuunch!"

"Lunch!" Donald Duk is outraged.

"Yes, lunch," the girl says.

"How many miles did we make?"

"What?" Mom asks. It's morning. The dim and bleak morning before warmth and sunbeams in the air. Hours before any sun. All over the walls are Donald Duk's aging movie posters and glossy stills from Fred Astaire's movies. Each Fred Astaire wrapped tight in shiny transparent plastic wrap makes a lot of strange eyes looking out of the shadows and the jittery shine of things in the room. Donald Duk realizes where he is and wants back into the dream. The dream is already nothing but a fading feeling. But how? And why? Donald Duk closes his eyes and covers his head with his pillow.

"What are you doing, dear?" Mom asks.

"I'm trying to remember."

"Oh, you were dreaming. Well, it's all gone now. Probably it's better that way. You don't want all that Freudian stuff getting in the way of your day. Did you dream too, Arnold?"

"I don't know," Arnold says, thinking hard, and squints back into his sleep. He wonders out loud. "Beaver hats? Rain on beaver hats?"

"They're wearing beaver hats in my dream too. And it's raining," Donald says.

Dad steps into the doorway, leaving Donald to wonder if Arnold Azalea dreams the same dreams of the railroad tracklaying contest every night he sleeps here. "Everybody still friends?" Dad asks big. "Get up!" He pulls the blankets off the boys and throws them on the floor. "One word of backtalk and I swear I'll take you to the herbalist and get you a bitter tea to make you straight! Hear me?" Dad says. His eyes look into Donald Duk's eyes for just an instant. The herbalist was a dream. No wonder Fred Astaire was just outside the door.

"Make the beds," Dad says. "Get washed and dress up, boys. Today is the third day of the new year, the Day of the Pig," Dad says, and walks on down the hall to work on his model planes while the boys dress and run to the five-thirty-in-the-morning tai chi.

"I'm sorry my father's such a pain," Donald Duk says after Mom and the twins leave the room.

"He seems okay to me," Arnold Azalea answers. "That's his friendly act."

"He seems to be a pretty good actor to me."

"A great actor! Your daddy's a great actor!" Uncle Donald Duk booms brassy, resonating and shimmering like a thumped gong above the meaty thunder of thousands of shod feet smacking and licking the streets of Chinatown early in the morning. "They say when your daddy wears the mask of Kwan Kung on stage, he is Kwan Kung himself, and he puts a big stop on all magic. I tell you Ah King was so great that when he comes out on stage, ghosts disappear from cemeteries, magician's saws cut through the beautiful ladies. Your daddy breaks spells and make everything too moochie real."

Dad snorts and looks across the street as he walks. The family, Arnold Azalea, Uncle Donald Duk and a gathering army from the opera company walk and chatter through Chinatown looking for breakfast. Pork chop and fried eggs at Sun Wah Kue on Washington. "You'll love it," Uncle Donald Duk says. "It has the old marble table tops and a marble floor. Good for keeping cool."

"You were really in Chinese opera, Daddy?" Venus asks.

"Ahhh. That's a long long time ago."

"Try and speak clearly in front of the children, King. What kind of example are you presenting, anyway?" Mom says.

"Your Daddy is just playing shy, kids. He wants to get onstage again. You want it, don't you Ah-King, ahhh!" Uncle Donald Duk says.

"Oh, why don't you? We would all love to see you on stage," Mom says.

"Oh, we would just love to," Venus says, wildly mimicking Mom. "Arrrrggh! Forget it."

"What kind of impression do you think you are making on Donald's friend?"

"We are not picking on you or anything, Daddy," Penny flutters her eyelashes and trills sweetly.

"Oh, no, Daddy, we would never do that!" Venus says.

"Never, never, never, never, never!" Penny says.

On the way to Sun Wah Kue Chinese-American Food, Dad stops by a row of plastic tubs filled with gray freshwater clams and live crawling crawdads, looking like miniature Maine lobsters, on a folding table set up by a parking meter in front of a Chinatown bank. The Crawdad Man's pickup truck is parked at the meter. The Crawdad Man wears a blue-visored yachting cap, a blue bandana around his neck, a canvas bib apron, black denim jeans and high-topped rubber boots. The Crawdad Man's son, Donald Duk's age, climbs out of the cab of the pickup dressed like his dad.

"Eh, Crawdad Man! Happy New Year! *Goong hay fot choy.*" Dad hands a red envelope of *lay see* to Crawdad Jr.

"Goong hay fot choy," Crawdad Jr. says.

"You know Duk, the opera Sifu," Dad says.

"Sure, I gave him a ride in from the airport. Happy New Year."

"Sure, sure. Have you eaten yet, Crawdad Man?" Uncle Donald Duk asks. "Here, son. *Goong hay fot choy,"* he says, handing a red envelope to the boy. "You minding you papa? Huh?"

"Your son has really grown, Crawdad Man," Mom says. "This is Arnold Azalea, Donald's friend. Introduce your friend, Donald."

"Uhhh, Uncle Crawdad Man, this is my friend Arnold Azalea. Arnold, this is the Crawdad Man, and his son, Crawdad Jr."

As they shake hands with the boys, Dad says, "Come on and have a little breakfast with us. We're going to Sun Wah Kue."

"Come on, Ah-King, I have a living to make. I'm no bigshot like you."

"Ha ha, don't listen to him, Arnold. He doesn't make his living selling this little truckload of clams and crawdaddies. He farms these critters with watercress and sells both by the hundreds of pounds!"

"Yeah, sure. I do this for fun! Here, Arnold, *Goong hay fot choy.* You too Donald, Happy New Year." The Crawdad Man hands each of the boys a red envelope of *lay see.* "Ha ha ha, Ah-Arnold. You stick with your Uncle King Duk, and you'll get rich, kid!"

"I am rich," Arnold says.

"Whoo! Rich already! Good. Ha ha. Ah-King, are we going to play Santa Claus this year?"

"Sure, sure. Of course," Dad says and shakes hands again with the Crawdad Man.

Early winter dusk over the Chinatown Branch Public Library. Donald Duk and Arnold run up wide stone stairs to a WPA pseudo-Grecian building with columns and brass doors. The doors are closed and locked . The boys turn and start down the stairs.

"What kind of book were you looking for?" a voice asks behind them, and there's a man with thin blond hair looking like long dried-out summer grass bending under the wind. The man is sun-tanned dark. His scalp is peeling and showing many colors of many varieties of fish flesh between the stalks of his straw hair. He wears a gray double-breasted suit and a brown tie.

"Something on the railroad," Donald Duk calls up the stairs to the straw-haired man.

"Something on the railroad? Not many Chinese are interested in reading about the railroad."

"We built them. So we might as well read about them."

"Oh, a wiseass too."

"Just a kid who thirsts for knowledge," Donald Duk says, smiling, and adds a sweet sugary "Sir."

"We open at ten in the morning."

"Wait! Just one question, please. Does the name or title *the Big Four* mean anything, when it comes to railroads?"

"The Big Four?" Strawhair sighs, looks down at the shine of his shoes, down at the traffic on Powell Street, then says, "The Big Four built the western half of the transcontinental railroad. The names of the Big Four are all over San Francisco. C. P. Huntington was a U.S. senator. Crocker, well, he liked to dress in white and ride a white horse along the track and watch the work. Mark Hopkins has a hotel named after him. Leland Stanford was governor of California and is the reason Leland Stanford University is named Leland Stanford University. And there you are! The mystery of the Big Four is solved."

"Thank you, sir. You have no idea how greatly you have enlightened me," Donald Duk says and goes on down the stairs with Arnold Azalea.

"Do you think you're going to dream again tonight?" Arnold asks.

After another simple family dinner for 250 at the restaurant, Uncle Donald Duk paints his finished wings. Mom watches and kibitzes Arnold's every move, glueing and pinning stringers across the bulkheads, finally starting construction of the model after cutting out all the pieces outlined in blue on the sheets of balsa wood, which is an Asian wood, people who know anything about wood are quick to say. Dad is carving the fuselage of a Grumman biplane out of a solid block of balsa wood, using plans he xeroxes and enlarges out of an ancient copy of *Model Airplane News*. The twins paint their GeeBee Racers. Dad gets up and switches on the TV and turns it to face him from the front room. A newscast comes on. Dad adjusts the color to make everyone look Chinese and sits down to carve balsa.

"I think I'll go to bed early tonight, Mom," Donald Duk says.

"You feeling okay?" Dad gruffs. "You got a fever? See if he has a fever, Mom."

"No, I don't need to see any herbalist, if that's what you're thinking. I'm just a little tired, that's all. Goodnight, everybody."

"Goodnight, dear," Mom says and looks over the table to read Dad's face.

"What's wrong with him?" Donald Duk hears Dad say low to Mom as he walks down the hall to his room.

"He can't stop dreaming," Arnold says.

Dad turns away from the news and puts down his balsa block and X-acto knife, and considers Arnold Azalea. "Haaaa!" Dad says. "I think you're right, young man . . . He likes dreaming better than being and doing. That's the way he watches TV. He finds some old movie on a late-night channel and lets some dead guy in black-and-white be him."

"Now, King, if you drink too much," Mom sings a sinister little warning that makes Venus and Penelope simultaneously sigh.

"Gee!" Venus says, "Mom! You sound just like Connie Chung . . ."

". . . doing her impression of Annette Funicello," Penny says in Venus's voice as if Venus hasn't stopped.

". . . doing her impression of Shirley Temple," Venus continues.

". . . saying *Don't you dare hurt my grandfather, You!*" Penny finishes.

"Oh, you two are just so jenny say kwah shampoo. Fifi fie fie fo fo fum!"

"Oh, I love the way Mom speaks Spittoon." Venus says.

"Oh, thank you," Penny says. "She learned her Spittoon from early morning instructional TV. You would love Mom, except she's been institutionalized in Fog Bank Bubble Gardens ever since Annette Funicello started anchoring the NBC weekend news."

". . . after publishing her secret Mickey Mouse Club diaries and getting her PhD in Journalism from Columbia," Venus continues.

"Now, girls. Do not try to confuse me. I and only I can tell you two apart no matter what you do. Right, Ah-King?"

"It's more than just dreaming, Mr. Duk."

"Uncle King. No Mr. Duk around here. Come on. It's the Chinese way. It won't hurt. No obligation, no deposit, no return," Mom says.

"Haaaal, stop badgering the boy and let him finish," Dad says. "Pardon me for interrupting you, young man. Please, finish what you were about to say."

"Sometimes I dream the same dreams."

"As Donald?" Venus asks. Arnold nods his head. "Oh," the twins say.

"Ah-Arnold, you are quite the mystic, aren't you," Mom says.

And Donald Duk dreams even as he asks over and over, "Why are we wasting a whole hour for lunch?" He sees Kwan the foreman riding in the locomotive cab with the hoghead and fireman, shoving a load of empties back to the terminal town, where thirteen other trains of rail are ready to shove to the end of track. "Does he have any idea of how long one hour is? Maybe another mile or more of track, right?"

"They ran out of track," the girl Donald Duk's age with the staff says.

"Now what?" Donald Duk asks.

"Now they go back for more."

During the break she begins to teach Donald Duk how to handle the staff. She makes it look easy. It isn't easy for Donald Duk. A few milling workers and children watch as they munch and slurp their lunch.

Kwan, the hoghead, the fireman and head end brakeman ride in the cab chugging and cooking backward, shoving the empty flatcars with the fuel tender still more than half full of wood. Crocker's grand plan of fourteen trains hot to highball has hit a glitch. The locomotive on the ground in yesterday's rain is still on the ground and jamming the mainline, like a piece of art. The piece of art fouls the lead tracks to the other thirteen trains on their thirteen tracks. The plan is to shove the empties off on a sidetrack and head back down the main to the train of loaded flatcars stranded on the main, pull them toward the end of the leads slowly, then get behind the loads by performing a chicken drop. What's a "chicken drop" Kwan wants to know.

13

KWAN THE FOREMAN follows the job conductor and a brakeman off the back of the locomotive onto the narrow grate of the fuel tender, rocking and clunking a load of firewood the Chinese had felled on the mountainsides while clearing the right of way. They hold onto an iron rod attached a few inches above their heads off the side of the tender car and sidestep along the narrow catwalk. The brakeman climbs closer to the wheels on the back of the tender. His hand is low, ready to grab the handle to the steel pin that holds the tender's coupling locked onto the coupling of their cut of empties. The conductor stands on the end, with one hand hanging onto an iron handhold. "Kwan," he says, "I want you to watch my right arm and hand. Whatever it does, you do with your arm and hand, understand?"

"You want me to pass signals."

"There's my good man. Pass signals it is. But exactly as I do, mind! The hoghead can read your hands as fine as any violinist reads his conductor's hands, and work this locomotive like a surgeon his knife, so pass the signals exact now."

The conductor points over the flat floors of the empty flatcars to the endless straight track of the mainline back to the Sierras. "Now do you see where the lead tracks branch off the main to the sidetracks there?" the conductor shouts. "The sidetracks are numbered from the mainline outward. See, there? The train off Track One snaked out onto the main and went on the ground, and you see the cocksucker there is fouling the way to Track Thirteen, trapping all them fine flatcars loaded with more than ten miles of rail. Now one of my fine brakemen will walk his ass down to the lead to Track One and open the switch off the main. We will then use some of these empties to drag the engine a bit away from its train, after uncoupling it, of course, then we shall all lay to levering the frozen loco and its tender off the track, then let the buzzards have them. We'll use the empties to shove the train of loaded flats farther back down the main, past the lead to Track One, and we'll leave it there while we haul these empties back and shove them down Track One and leave them there, with the brakes tied on. With me so far, Kwan?"

"Fine! We get rid of the dead hog and our dozen empties," Kwan the foreman says. "But we are still ahead of the load, and we should be behind the cut of loaded cars to put the rails into my gangs' hands, right?"

"Thus, the great Lord of the Railroads did giveth unto the Brotherhood of Trainmen working the tricks of trains and tracks the wondrous Chicken Drop. After we kick the empties down Track One, we're taking the hog back up the main and chugging back down to the main. We shove it a bit farther down the track, stoke up a load of steam and then pull like the devil. On my signal, the hoghead brakes a little, the couplings crumple loose a moment, we pull the pin and race away with the hog. A brave brakeman stays on the loads, slowing them a little, as we pull past the points of the switch to Track One. At that point, as we pass, you throw the switch closed. We reverse down the lead. As soon as we're clear, you throw the switch open again.

"Now listen carefully. As soon as the cut of loaded flats passes, you throw the switch closed again. We will move this big iron hog up behind the train and grab it with our front couple. You open the switch again to the main and trot yourself back to the cab for the ride back to break that record, hear me?"

Kwan the foreman knows the brakeman's daylight hand signals, "Come to me," "Go away from me," "Stop," and the night signals with the lantern. But he has never seen the signal for a Chicken Drop.

The conductor stands on the ground, where the engineer can always see him along the main. The move is dangerous. The brakeman on the tender car knows to pull the pin when he feels the couplings give and hang on, as the loco, free of the weight, will grab for speed right away.

Kwan stands by the switchstand, opening and closing the switch points from the lead track to Track One to the mainline. The main has to stay open the way it is for the locomotive and tender to roll by. Kwan has unlocked the handle to the switchstand and pulled the lock, so come the time he has to lift the handle and crank it around to move the points closed and open the lead to let the locomotive back down toward Track One, he's ready.

The country's flat out here. Desert. The ground kicks the heat of the day back up into his feet, up into his face. The iron of the switch handle is hot. The engine is far enough down the main for Kwan to hear the birds and the high wind blowing invisibly through the clear sunshine. The monotonous flat ground and sky all around him are still unexpected, still a little frightening after all these weeks. He likes the nights. The quiet then, covering the crowd in the *deem sum* compound and the snores and gambling in the gangs' camp. He catches sight of the conductor signaling to the engine, with his yellow leather mitts gripped in his right hand. "Highball" is the signal. The conductor is calling for more speed. Kwan hears the clattering of the wheels, the peculiar ping and screech of stretching rail agonizing on the rolling flatcars. Now the conductor bends his knees, sits a little with his butt out, bends his elbows, tucks his hands into his armpits and flaps his arms, and mimics a chicken, then waves behind with his mittens. The locomotive slows just a little, and Kwan hears the crumpling of the big iron knuckles of the couplings as the grunt and crash begins. All seem rolling together still when first the train slows, then the engine breaks away down the main toward Kwan. The conductor runs toward Kwan's switch. The loco and tender pass Kwan, very hot, very humid, smelling of warm grease and oil, hot iron. Kwan throws the switch. The round target facing the oncoming traffic on the main is red, the lantern facing the track is red, the switch points are closed. The loco stops and seems to lean before muscling its way backward. Back toward Kwan the loaded flatcars drift close. Kwan sees them. Kwan feels their weight crunching down on the crossties, thumping them hard into the roadbed and ground under his feet. The engine and loaded flats roll toward each other, the engine racing suicidally it seems, then it passes onto the lead past Kwan. He throws the switch to let the flats roll down the main without braking them. They pass him slowly, singing. Kwan throws the switch again and the loco and tender move off the lead onto the main behind the drifting train. Kwan quickly sets the switch, locks it up and runs.

Dancing the lion, working the staff, Donald Duk feels them in his wrists. They throb. He drops his arms and pants for breath. The girl Donald Duk's age does a few of Monkey's moves with the staff. "How far have we come, anyway?" Donald Duk asks.

"Six miles from sunrise till one o'clock, when we stopped for lunch," she answers.

"Six miles. We're going to beat their eight miles, aren't we! We're really going to do it. The World Record!"

Chief Engineer Strobridge has his eye to the eyepiece of his brass transit on a tripod. A reporter peers through a telescope. "Six miles! The Celestials seem to have set themselves an extraordinary pace. How do you make them do it, Mr. Strobridge?"

"To be perfectly truthful, sir, they have too much pride to work for me. I do not make them do a thing. 'Tis not in my power," Strobridge says.

"It is then a tribute to your superior organization of the coolie labor, Mr. Strobridge. Six miles! Brilliant organization of 400 small, weak . . ."

"Whoa, sir. Not weak."

"Nonetheless, a heathen race versus 400 hot-tempered, individualistic Christian Irish who love nothing more than a yard of beer and a brawl. It is clear to me superior generalship of inferior troops will triumph over inferior generalship of superior troops."

Kwan steps into the scope of Strobridge's transit. Strobridge follows him. Kwan carries a length of smoldering rope in his hand. He comes to the fuse of a large rocket. "Kwaaan," Strobridge mutters in anticipation.

The reporter with the telescope asks, "By the way, what are the names of the eight Irishmen unloading the rail?"

Kwan lights the fuse, the rocket goes off leaving a trail of sparks and explodes. Work starts.

The crossties thump off the wagons and stomp into the roadbed. The tampers tamp, the rails clang, the tongs clink and ting and the rail sings as steel tools set and gauge. Then the hammers hammer, the pike bites home and the rail sings fishplates and nuts and bolts wrenched tight with tools as long as a man is tall, made of solid steel that gets hot in the sun, hot with the work and cooled by the grease and sweat of the handlers. They're only a little bigger than Donald, only a couple of years older. The faces are so young. They wear black. If they comb their hair differently and put on dark glasses, they'd look like gang kids in Chinatown.

In and out from inside the lion's head, he dances and kicks after the girl. She makes dangerous scary moves at the lion, pokes and whacks with her staff pretty as the flight of a hummingbird. Donald Duk feels his heart thumping, galloping easy, and his eyes seeing everything a little crazy. All day chasing the thump of the drum over the ground shuddering under his feet. He is thinking and feeling like the lion he is dancing, and he feels a little dangerous himself. The shadow of the lion is long and distinct on the ground, stretching away from his feet. He feels a faint breeze lick up his back. The dust kicked up by all the work turns into a bright cloud of flaming yellow and rust as the sun goes low.

Strobridge and the reporters and artists move ahead of the work, pitch camp and start fires that burn large and bright as the work is splashed with the colors and shadows of sunset, then the sky goes dark.

A jet of steam shoots wet and white up from the drooling steam whistle on the locomotive, and its long, monstrous, eagle-like scream fills this particular hollow of the ancient seabed, announcing the end of the workday. The end of the try for The World Record. And all the steel goes silent and leaves a ringing in Donald Duk's ears.

At the very end of the last rail laid, a surveyor's helper stands among the milling Chinese holding a colored pole. A fire burns nearby, throwing moments of light on him. Strobridge focuses his transit on a target on the helper's pole and writes in a bound notebook with a pencil. Kwan the foreman stands next to Strobridge and glances at the bearded chief engineer and superintendent's figuring. Donald Duk and Yin the Wrestler's Kung fu family stand near the fire at the end of the track.

"A rail is forty feet long. You figure the number of rails we laid, times forty, then you divide by two, " Kwan mutters to Strobridge, who stops writing in his notebook to throw Kwan a look.

"Why divide by two?" a reporter asks.

"To allow for using half of all the rails laid for the other side of the track. Am I right, Kwan?"

"Or figure the number of rails laid, times twenty, and save dividing by two," Kwan says.

"And we will have the length of track we laid down to the foot," Strobridge finishes.

The end of track is now a tourist park. Large campfires burn everywhere around the end of track. Servants unload and set up tables and chairs, then set the tables. Cooks cook at the woodfires. Liveried servants attend the set tables. In front of the line of camps, Crocker on his white horse paces back and forth like a guardian between the Chinese workgangs and the people who matter to him, the tourists.

The tourists see the locomotive outline by the fires and the last light in the western sky. They see milling workers outlined against their huge fires. The loco's whistle blasts for attention.

The blast seeps into the night. Kwan the foreman's voice rises in the cold, carries and fades on the breeze. "Ten miles, one thousand two hundred feet!" he calls. "Ten miles, twelve hundred feet! World Record!"

A cheer and a clatter of tools rises from the gangs. Firecrackers. Lion drums. Gongs and cymbals. Then distant thunder stomps and rumbles in the west. Crocker backs his white horse up to the missionary in collar and buckskins translating by Strobridge's tent, "What did he say?" Crocker asks.

"World Record," the missionary translator says.

"How many miles, man? How many miles?"

"Ten miles," the missionary says.

"Ten miles!" Crocker says and pulls himself back into the saddle.

"Twelve hundred feet," the missionary translates.

"Ten miles, twelve hundred feet!" Crocker whoops. He rears his horse and waves his white hat. "Ten miles, twelve hundred feet!"

The tourists look beyond the prancing Crocker to the glow rising from the railhead. A cloud boils from the west and pancakes low over the workers around the railhead. The tourists see from their campsites, their cookfires, their supper tables lightning striking in the cloud.

A weird cloud. Low. Very low, too low for a thundercloud, but there it is. Kwan looks up to the western sky and Donald sees the foreman's face come to light in a lightning strike. The air is very close. Lightning is all over the western sky. "A dragon's claw," Kwan says low. "Thunder from the Sierra." The thunder does not stop; it is the gallop of 108 horses out of the west, over the track. Clouds roll and boil ahead of the galloping horses and riders, clearly visible now, over the track. Ahead of the 108, Kwan Kung gallops his horse Red Rabbit up to the end of track, twirling his halberd. He reins Red Rabbit up, opens his mouth to a thunder-clap and gallops on as the thunder of the 108 horses and riders rolls closer. Donald Duk knows Kwan Kung's face. It is as red as the pictures and statues he sees all over Chinatown, all over his mem-ory of visiting the Chinese restaurants of Dad's friends. Opera people.

The thunder is right overhead now, and Donald Duk looks up into the cloud. Horsemen and flags announce the Thirty-six Stars of Heavenly Spirits, armored and girded for war, accompanied by their banners and pennants followed by the Seventy-two Stars of Earthly Fiends, fancy names for outlaws and rebels against the Song Empire. These are the famous outlaws of Leongshan Marsh that Dad is painting on his 108 model planes, and Uncle Donald Duk says he should know, because everybody knows the 108 out-laws of the marsh like they know the three brothers of the oath of the peach garden, like they know Robin Hood, Spider-Man, Bat-man and Robin. The outlaws dismount. Donald sees a woman wearing two swords across her back, with the handles gleaming just above her shoulders. The outlaws stride to the edge of the cloud and look down as if looking over the edge of the Grand Can-yon. They cover their right fists with their left hands in a salute. Then they break into applause and grins.

Lee Kuey, a dark-haired, big-shouldered orangutan of a man, is naked. He stomps to the edge with a huge battle-axe in each hand. He paces along the edge of the cloud, looking into every face with his fierce crazy eyes.

"Who are they?" Donald Duk asks.

"You don't know them?" the girl his age asks, full of surprise and a little suspicious. He's surprised himself. He knows them. He knows them, so why does he ask in his dream?

"I have only heard about them. I don't know what they look like. I'm from San Francisco, not China."

"You were born here, boy?" she asks.

"Yeah," Donald Duk says.

"Oooh!" everyone in Yin the Wrestler's Kung fu family says, amazement in their eyes. A Chinaman, Donald Duk's age, born and raised in American in 1867!

Lee Kuey stops on the edge of the cloud just above Donald Duk and shakes his battle-axes at him. "Hey you! Frisco punk!" A lightning bolt strikes short of Donald Duk but still knocks him on his butt.

"You better remember me!" Lee Kuey talks in a voice of crunching gravel, "Cuz I am out to get ya! I have the blood of punks like you drying into scabs all over my body!"

"Ah-Lee Kuey!" a dark, pot-bellied man in blue says. "Leave the boy alone. One of these days you are going to go too far! Don't think I won't . . . !"

"Please don't say that," Lee Kuey says and drops to his knees and crosses his battle-axes across his chest. "Please, brother, don't say it."

"Get out of my sight! And stay sober!" the short dark man says, and steps closer to the edge of the cloud and points to Donald Duk. "You!"

Donald Duk looks up, and everyone near him steps away.

"I am a man of no talent, boy. That is why I value what little knowledge of the talented and gallant I possess. I have been fortunate enough to hold a small official position in a humble county seat at a major crossroads of the empire, and have accumulated a small reputation among all the brave, the talented, the gallant and incorruptible everywhere as a fair friend in hard times.

"You have no reason to remember anyone as ignorant and without skills as myself. But you would do me a great honor if when the world turns harsh against the honest and incorruptible, you look me up before you sell out. My name is Soong Gong. These fighters know me by my nickname: the Timely Rain."

The gangs all look up in awe at the 108 and strain to hear the words of Soong Gong. "I say that to all of you," Soong Gong says. The Chinese are sweating and still panting for breath after their race with hammers and rails. Soong Gong gestures, and a misty rain slowly falls from his hand and the cloud, and it is cool cool on the skin and makes the air sweet to breathe, and the mist falls and cools as Soong Gong remounts and leads the 108 galloping back toward the Sierras.

Donald Duk wakes up dreaming of the wind through the tops of the pine trees in the Sierras. Kwan wants to see him. Donald Duk finds the foreman hunkering on his heels by a fire.

"Hey, Frisco Kid! You know how to sign your name in Chinese?" Kwan asks. "We want you to sign something."

"What?"

Kwan points at a crosstie. Chinese names are carved all over it. "That will be the last crosstie. We cut it out of California laurel. It is the last crosstie we Chinese will lay building this transcontinental railroad. Everyone who works the right of way puts their name on, see? So all our names will mark exactly how far we came from Sacramento."

Donald Duk looks the last crosstie over. A young man loads a brush with black ink and writes his name on a face of the tie. He passes the brush, blows on the ink to dry it and starts carving his name. The crosstie is covered with names. Some carved. Some just written in ink. A young man holds the brush out to Donald Duk. Donald Duk hesitates. He does not know what to say, or what he wants to say.

"Are you ashamed of laying The World Record, boy?" Kwan the foreman asks.

"Ashamed of setting a world record?" Donald Duk asks back, and reaches for the brush.

Wham! Air blasts into his ear. Explosion! He hears the twins shouting "Wake up! Wake up! Tai chi time! Tai chi in the morning!" as they whomp him over the head with pillows. He's awake. His friend Arnold Azalea is awake. The twins are running for their room and gone.

14

DONALD DUK DREAMS he's sleeping at night and wakes up dreaming, and wakes up from that dream into another, and wakes up into the real.

Morning in San Francisco Chinatown. The clammy milky light before dawn collects in the tissue-paper skins of Dad's model planes hanging from the ceiling, and they glow like Chinese lanterns. Pieces of the balsa wood skeleton of the P-26A Donald is building to replace the one he still remembers burning over Chinatown lie assembled and pinned to the plans laid out on his worktable. The planes seem to move as he passes the doorway to the dining room. He feels like he's still a character in his dream and expects to wake up just one more time. Is this another dream when he sees the girl his age with the staff at the White Crane Club? No. It's a tubby boy with glasses and braces.

On the way home, at a trot with Arnold Azalea, Donald Duk does not feel all here. There is a peculiar silly stillness about Chinatown. He walks home by streets and through alleys he does not usually walk. Everything is closed this early in the morning. Cold darkness inside every shop. Cold light. A book-and-magazine store is open in an alley.

Strange. The lights are on bright. The doors are open. A Chinese woman wearing a buttoned-up sweater sits on a high stool behind a cash register. A lookout for a gambling den? No. The gamblers go home before first light. They are all asleep and dreaming, not to wake up till noon or later.

No one is surprised Donald Duk and Arnold Azalea step inside to browse this early in the morning. A cat pads between the rows of books. Donald Duk faces a wall of softbound multi-volume sets of comic books telling the stories of *The Three Kingdoms,* and *The Water Margin, Monkey's Journey to the West, The Seven Women Generals of the Yang Family* and other heroic tales with bows and arrows, swords and slings, spears and horses. Donald Duk slides open the box reading *Characters in Water Margin Playing Cards. Made in Shanghai, China.* Two full decks of cards inside. One with red backs. One with blue backs. Full-length portraits of the characters of the popular novel are on the playing-card faces. Each deck has four suits with ace, king, queen, jack, two through ten, and three jokers. One of the red jokers is the man who stopped Lee Kuey from throwing a battle-axe through Donald Duk. The peach-colored robe. The long trailing feathers, like the long trailing pheasant feathers on the headdresses of Aztec warriors on the calendars in Mexican restaurants. "Arnold! Come here! Here he is."

"Who?"

"The Timely Rain, he called himself," Donald takes the red joker to the woman knitting behind the cash register. "Can you tell me who this is?" he asks.

The woman glances at the card. "Why, that's Soong Gong. So, who did you think it was?"

"Who is Soong Gong?"

"Who is Soong Gong?" the woman laughs, "Come on, boy!"

The door behind the cash register opens. A medium tall man in a black three-piece suit and a black hat steps into the doorway. He slips a coiled black bullwhip over his shoulder. He focuses his eyes on Donald Duk, and Donald Duk doesn't like it. He feels himself coming apart being seen by this man.

"Come on, Ah-Bok, people here don't wear hats anymore. And that bullwhip, I'm surprised they let you on the plane with such a terrible thing," the woman says.

The man with the bullwhip yawns and slips a large round gold pocketwatch out of his vest pocket, and drops it back in. "I'm a detective sergeant of the Honolulu Police Department. People on the plane are happy I carry my bullwhip, and my gun too, by dammit."

"Watch your language in front of this boy, Charlie. *Wuhay!* He doesn't know who Soong Gong is."

"What's that you say?" and the bullwhip snaps his eyes on Donald Duk again. Donald Duk shows the card to Sgt. Bullwhip and asks, "Who's this? She says his name is Soong Gong. I think he's called the Timely Rain. So who is he?"

"He's the leader of the 108 outlaws. Name Soong Gong. Nickname him: Timely Rain. Don't you know that, boy? Every boy and girl knows that. Why don't you? You some kind of dimwit? Everything a little foggy to you?"

Donald Duk shows Sgt. Bullwhip from Honolulu the card showing the dark naked man with a battle-axe in each hand. "Who's this?"

"Why, that's Lee Kuey. They call him the Black Tornado, because he is ugly, bad-tempered and cuts through fighting men like a buzzsaw. This guy is crazy in the cabeza. He kills as many of his friends by accident as bad guys. But he's so good at it, understand me? You never heard of him? So why do you ask?"

"Where are you from, boy?" the woman asks. "You a Chinatown kid?"

"Yeah . . ."

"How come you don't know these guys?" the woman asks, buttoning her buttons again. "Do you know who this old man is?"

"No."

"This is Charlie Chan."

"Charlie Chan?" Donald Duk asks and looks at the man without looking into the man's eyes. "He's not fat enough to be Charlie Chan."

"The real Charlie Chan," the woman says. "His family name is Chang. In Hawaii they call him Chang Apana."

"Sergeant Chang Apana," Bullwhip says.

"He's famous just famous for keeping the peace on Hotel Street in the twenties. Aren't you, Ah-Bok?"

"I keep the peace at the baseball too," Bullwhip says. "Get him a copy of that poster picture of the 108 outlaws." He points at the characters appearing lined up on the banks of a river or lake as the woman unrolls the poster. "There, you see, here's Soong Gong. And here's the Black Tornado. Ugly fella, huh! Stupid too. Loyal. Righteous too. Bad combination."

"That's just the way I saw them!" Donald Duk says. The 108 outlaws are lined up on the riverbank the way they were on the edge of the cloud. He pulls money out of his pocket to buy the poster, but Bullwhip won't let the woman roll the poster up and wrap it. "See here, this one. Sagacious Lowe. Wanted murderer becomes this Buddhist monk. Eats meat. Drinks booze. Beats people up. Breaks statues of Buddha up. Too devout to live in a monastery. Ha ha. And this one's Tiger Killer Jung. One by one all these fella join up with Soong Gong in the Water Margin. This is the one guy who is not jealous. He give you a helping hand in good times or bad times. When I'm a kid like you, I daydream someday someone from Leongshan Marsh—that one Marvelous Traveler—find me and say, *The Timely Rain says he is man no talent, but he's seen lots of war. He longtime admire your bravery. Soong Gong asks you to join him and his gang of outlaw heroes in Leongshan Marsh. Before you lie. Before you betray. Before you sell out . . .* But you grow up. You sell out. You lie. Just a little bit, maybe you cheat on your wife, no good, and think it is just little bit, but too much to ever expect the Marvelous Traveler to come up with that message from the Timely Rain . . ."

"If you're the real Charlie Chan, how do you solve murder mysteries?"

"I got my bullwhip."

"For solving murders?"

"And for crowd control too," Sgt. Bullwhip says.

DONALD DUK AND ARNOLD AZALEA are the only people in the huge marble reading room of the main library. "Here it is!" Donald Duk whispers.

"Me too," Arnold says, reading from a book on top of a pile of closed books, "I found it too. *Thursday, April* 29, 1869*.*"

Donald Duk reads from the book on top of his stack of closed books, "Listen to this: *Each man in Strobridge's astonishing team of tracklayers had lifted* 125 *tons of iron in the course of the day. The consumption of materials was even more impressive.* 25,800 *ties.* 3,520 *rails,* 28,160 *spikes,* 14,800 *bolts . . .* "

"Wow," Arnold whispers.

"Listen to this: *As soon as the epic day's work was done, Jim Campbell, who later became a division superintendent for the C.P., ran a locomotive over the new track at forty miles an hour to prove the record-breaking feat was a sound job as well.* Does it say anything about Kwan in any of your books?"

"I don't see anything yet," Arnold says.

"Look at this: *At rail's end stood eight burly Irishmen, armed with heavy track tongs. Their names were Michael Shay, Patrick Joyce, Michael Kennedy, Thomas Dailky, George Elliot, Michael Sullivan, Edward Killeen, and Fred McNamara.* Not one Chinese name. We set the record and not one of our names. Not one word about our last crosstie." Donald Duk whispers in the library.

And while working on his model P-26A Peashooter at home, he says, "We made history. Twelve hundred Chinese. And they don't even put the name of our foreman in the books about the railroad."

"So what?" Dad asks.

Donald Duk doesn't say a word back.

Dad catches Donald Duk's eye. "What're you look at me that way for? Fix your face."

"Didn't you hear what I said?" Donald Duk asks.

"They don't want our names in their history books. So what? You're surprised. If we don't write our history, why should they, huh?"

"It's not fair."

"Fair? What's fair? History is war, not sport! You think if you are a real good boy for them, do what they do, like what they like, get good grades in their schools, they will take care of you forever? Do you believe that? You're dreaming, boy. That is faith, sincere belief in the goodness of others and none of your own. That's mysticism. You believe in the goodness of others to cover your butt, you're good for nothing. So, don't expect me to get mad or be surprised the *bokgwai* never told our history in any of their books you happen to read in the library, looking for yourself. You gotta keep the history yourself or lose it forever, boy. That's the mandate of heaven."

15

"WHAT DO YOU MEAN, the mandate of heaven?" Donald Duk asks. "I know, I know, I asked before. But I'm really listening this time. Really, I'm listening very carefully."

"The mandate of heaven. Hmmmm."

"Listen to your father, girls, and learn," Mom says.

"They don't tell you the mandate of heaven in Chinese school?" Dad asks. "You know, *tien ming.*"

Donald Duk does not say he does not go to Chinese school anymore. "Mr. Meanwright says the mandate of heaven means the emperor is all-powerful and gets his power from God in heaven, like the divine right of kings in Europe."

"Nah." Uncle Donald Duk snorts.

"Nah?" Donald Duk says.

"Nah! That's nothing Chinese," Uncle Donald Duk says.

"Haaaaa!" Dad speaks a weary roar, "I told you! Ah-tien ming, mandate of heaven, is Confucius. Confucius says to the king, to the emperor, *Watch out! Your power is going to corrupt you. Pervert your princes and make outlaws of the honest people and your rotten dynasty will die nasty for sure.* Kingdoms rise and fall. Nations come and go. That's the mandate of heaven."

"That's the mandate of heaven?" Arnold asks.

Dad turns and Donald sees his eyes. "Daaad!" Donald Duk says with a smile. "Arnold asked that, not me! " He throws up two fingers in a V, the old peace sign, "Peace, brother! Right on, far owooot!" Wow! When the twins aren't here, he invents them.

"You know how you have to talk pretty language to the emperor. Like, you do not say *peepee doodoo* to the President of the United States," Uncle Donald Duk says in an easy happy voice. "Confucius just can't say what they call *the will of the people*. The emperor or someone who wants to be emperor only talks the language if he's the Son of Heaven and tells all living things what to do. So Confucius calls the will of the people *heaven.*"

"Like in my restaurants," Dad says, "I don't say *sliced cross-section of broccoli spear alternate with slices of Virginia ham and chicken breast.* Sounds too laboratory science. Who wants to eat some kind of autopsy? Ugh! So, I say *Jade Tree Golden Smoke Ham and Chicken.* In Chinese, oh, it sounds even more beautiful. *Yuke shur gum wah faw tur gai kow.* Jade tree. Sounds so pretty you don't feel bad about paying too much money to eat broccoli."

Dad holds a plane up to the light, which casts the shadows of cherry bombs and fuses he's mounted on the wing spars on the paper skin of the wings. "Poetry is strategy, you see? Strategy."

Donald Duk is warm, even now when it's foggy and wet outside late, walking in the shadows with Fred Astaire. Donald and Fred dance a little. They walk a little. The wet streets and fog add a razzling echo to their taps, dancing and walking. "I ask him a question and I get double talk. He treats Arnold Azalea better than me. I don't think he's setting me a good example at all."

"Fathers are hard to understand when you're the son," Fred Astaire says.

"I have always dreamed of being like you. Did you ever dream of being like me?"

"Oh, no. I have always dreamed of being Fred Astaire. No one knows my real name anymore."

"Fred Astaire's not your real name, Fred?"

"I can't be certain after all these years being Fred Astaire, and all these conflicting reports and rumors and affidavits . . . but if you ask around, I'm sure somebody, some fan or cinema buff, will know for sure what my real name is if it isn't Fred Astaire."

"All that matters to you is you are what you always dreamed you'd be."

"If you forget who you are in your dreams, maybe, then maybe, that is what dreams are for." Fred mingles away with a gaggle of reporters, telling jokes.

Two locomotives and tenders face each other head-on over an expanse of bare roadbed. The Central Pacific Railroad from the west is about to link up with the Union Pacific Railroad from the east. The Central Pacific and Union Pacific have each built side tracks along the unfinished right of way and parked their elegant private cars and party cars on siding. Donald Duk knows this is Promontory Point. Dust. No one would know it had rained heavily here a few days ago. The dust comes from the feet of moving men. The Central Pacific Engine No. 60, the "Jupiter," shines and gleams brass and polished paint as if it isn't here at all. The Jupiter is a huge Christmas toy of a locomotive to Donald Duk's eye.

In Crocker's private car, Charles Crocker of the Central Pacific and the bearded Casement brothers, Jack and Dan, of the Union Pacific finish off a tense laugh, a civil cigar and a whiskey. Crocker in his white frock coat and riding breeches. The Casement brothers in their dark suits. They glimpse the forms of four Chinese trotting past with an unusually decorated crosstie on their shoulders. "Now what the hell is this?" Crocker says, swallowing the lingering taste of whiskey and stepping to the window. He puts down his glass and grabs his hat. "The Celestials never cease to amaze me."

Donald Duk is caught up, running with the Chinese gangs to get close to the last tie, to shoulder it and run with it. Donald Duk looks back and forth for Kwan the foreman and sees Crocker and Union Pacific Vice President T.C. Durant, looking something like the owl on *Sesame Street* and something like a goat, and the Casement brothers climbing into a horsedrawn buggy. The Casement brothers look like the Smith brothers on Smith Brothers cough drops boxes.

The gangs come to a stop at the bed for the last crosstie, Kwan orders the men holding the tie to raise it above their heads so everyone can see the names. "They asked who can stuff dynamite and nitro six feet into a two-inch hole with a steel bar a hundred feet up a sheer rock face, and the *bokgwai* said they can't do it. And the Chinamans say we are men of no talent but have seen much blasting. And the Chinamans blasted. They asked who can carve the mountains with hand tools. We carved the mountains. They asked who can live inside tunnels in the snow. They asked who can lay ten miles of track in one day. They bet $10,000 we can't lay more than seven. We lay ten miles, twelve hundred feet of track in ten hours. One foot for every Chinaman who ever worked building this railroad. Your names are here. This is how far we have come from Sacramento."

They lay the crosstie into the gravel right of way, tamp it and spike rail into it. Firecrackers go off, and the Chinese jump and make a show of stepping on the tie, do a dance on it, hop on it with one foot and wander back to camp.

Donald Duk lingers at the site, and is still here, studying the tie covered with the names of 10,000 Chinese on all sides and the ends, when the hatted and spatted railroad executives dismount their buggy and step up for a look. Men from the Union Pacific crews and a few reporters, sketch artists and sightseers come out for tomorrow's last spike ceremony slowly drift through the heat to see what brings the railroad barons out of their private cars.

Crocker and the black-bearded Casement brothers in black coats look, to everybody, like they're going to fight. The race to be the first to Promontory and win a huge government bonus has not been friendly. The government has declared both winners to stop the railroads' trading acts of increasingly violent sabotage.

Crocker's Central Pacific is not happy. The Union Pacific's Jack Casement and his brother are not satisfied. There's no taking it away from the Irish for the Chinese and vice versa. The reporters in celluloid collars, the sketch artists with their flicking, skeptical eyes and flurry of hands and the telegraph operators dog their every move outside their private cars. The too dapper, too San Francisco snooty, good-time Charlie Crocker would love to see himself written large in *Harper's Weekly,* or Frank Leslie's *IllustratedMagazine,* crossing the Sierra Nevadas like an American Alexander the Great or Napoleon, sneaking their armies over the Alps. A double-page steel engraving picturing him in white on his white horse, leading his army of Chinese and the beauty among locomotives, the Jupiter, over the Sierras.

The sadistic Jack Casement pushed his Union Pacific crews along with his bullwhip, whiskey and rolling bawdyhouses in box cars. He dresses like a preacher of doom and silently but otherwise openly shows he thinks Crocker is a namby pamby windbag. Durant speaks for the Union Pacific and keeps Jack Casement awed into quiet by the history the dignitaries and writers and artists are making of every word they say, every look they exchange. Outside of their private cars, and even inside, every word they say reaches for future quotation.

"What is this?" Crocker asks.

"Our last crosstie," Donald Duk answers.

"Where did you learn to speak English, boy?" T.C. Durant asks.

"I was born in San Francisco."

"The greater number of my boys should speak some kind of English," Crocker says. "I am told your stalwart Irishmen do likewise." The onlookers laugh.

"Charlie, your railroad seems to hire a smaller and younger breed of laborer than mine," T. C. Durant says.

"Do you speak Chinese?" Donald Duk asks, looking up into Durant's face.

"Are you addressing me?" Durant asks. "Unfortunately, no! I am an American, sir . . ." he clears his throat, ". . . young man."

"Me, too, Mr. Durant. I was born here."

"Now don't you be rude and sassy, boy," Crocker says. "He probably belongs to one of the families that follow the Celestials and sell them food and medicine. We realize great savings with the Chinese over white laborers by providing them with a food allowance instead of the usual kitchens and cook's quarters on wheels. Your commissary unit and everything else you provide your crews with on wheels must cost a fortune."

"Still and all, we have presented us here a most remarkable example of the breed. He speaks English like a white man. Tell me, son, what exactly are all these chicken scratches and scrawlings on that crosstie?"

"They're our names, Mr. Durant."

"He certainly knows your name. Do you know mine, too, young man?" Crocker asks. "You should!"

"Of course. You're Charlie Crocker," Donald Duk says.

"You say those are your names," Crocker lurches on.

"All of our names. Ten thousand names."

"Why? "

"We don't want anyone to forget who laid these crossties and spiked this track."

". . . and built this railroad?" T. C. Durant coaxes with a sly eye toward the writers and artists.

". . . and built this railroad," Donald Duk says.

"You are just a little boy. You are too young to understand how history is made," Crocker turns to his chief engineer and superintendent. "Mr. Strobridge, I wish to tear out and split this crosstie with Mr. Durant of the Union Pacific as a sign of my respect and the joint achievements of our great railroads. Will you see to the tie's extraction and splitting, please."

"I'm sorry, Mr. Crocker, I cannot do that."

"Please, excuse me, Mr. Crocker, but if you will allow me, Mr. Strobridge," the bearded Jack Casement turns to his bearded Central Pacific counterpart, "I believe I understand your dilemma.

You have come many hard-worked miles with the Celestials, whose work has most assuredly accrued to your glory. But they don't work for Jack Casement, and my men can tear out that Chinese crosstie without disturbing the placid surface of our Christian consciences. And the Union Pacific will be glad to replace this tie with one *you* provide us, as a gesture . . ."

"How magnanimous of you, Jack! They called your worktrain *Hell on Wheels,* I hear. And you carried a bullwhip."

"Out here, everyone—man, woman and child—is either a muleskinner or a mule, Charlie. You know that. And the only difference between the muleskinner and the mule is the muleskinner's got the whip."

"Jack, please, I beg you, take your pick of any of those fine California pine ties I have stacked there . . ." Crocker says.

And Donald Duk is running a rage, gnashing his teeth, hardening his eyes to see fast and slow time down. Long before he can shout to Kwan and be heard, Donald sees Kwan the foreman hunkered down on the ground, playing Chinese chess on a blanket with a large railroader. Now and then they pick up teacups. A small group circles round to watch the game and eat out of bowls with chopsticks. Donald feels so close, the air is so clear, he is seeing so fast, still, all he can hear of what he sees are a few rattles and clangs from the *deem sum* people's cooking and serving. Even now, he still cannot be sure he hears the gambling and gaming he sees. He catches his breath on the run and shouts, "They're tearing out the tie! They're tearing out the tie!"

Crocker, Durant, the Casement brothers are at the front of a crowd of curious railroad bigwigs, engineers, surveyors watching the Union Pacific crew spike rail into the new last crosstie, and hear the Chinese running toward them, throwing rocks and screaming so fierce and intense the bigwigs back off.

Kwan leads the Chinese in grabbing the steel rails over the last crosstie with their bare hands and pulling them up, exposing several ties. They grab the new pine tie out of its socket and beat it against the discarded rails. The Chinese walk away with their hands clutching splinters of the pine tie. When Donald Duk looks over his shoulder at the bigwigs' crowd, he sees he is the last Chinaman, and not a trace of the pine tie left.

Crocker and the Union Pacific officers are stunned. "Governor Stanford will be attending tomorrow's ceremonies with his party from California, standing on this very spot," Crocker says.

"And I reckon twenty or thirty newspapers and magazines have sent their writers and artists. The Union Pacific, for our part, does not need another scandal," T. C. Durant says.

"Your candor is most refreshing and appreciated, sir. I promise you, Mr. Durant, there will not be a heathen in sight at tomorrow's ceremonies. I will, with your permission, post riflemen up on the locomotives and the telegraph poles to warn us of the approach of any uninvited Celestials and keep them away, with force of arms if need be. The Golden Spike. The Silver Spike. The Last Spike will be hammered home, the telegram sent, our photograph made to preserve a great moment in our nation's history, without the Chinese. Admire and respect them as I do, I will show them who built the railroad. White men. White dreams. White brains and white brawn."

16

ARE THERE ANY CHINESE in the old photos snapped at Promontory on May 10, 1869? One Chinese face? One glimpe of a long black braid of hair? Are the dreams so much poisoned poof? If there are none, does it mean the dreams are flashbacks to the real, to his ancestral first Lee come to America as a paper Duk? Is he this young, just Donald Duk's age, when he comes to America alone and sees the Chinese set the tracklaying record and signs his name to the last crosstie? He has the books with the pictures from the library. Big books. Big old pictures. He sees Chinese in the pictures snapped on May 8th.

It's an old photo of the Chinese coming back to tear out the tie that replaced theirs. On May 10th, the day of the last spike, the sledge used to drive the spike was wired to the telegraph to send the strike instantly to Washington. None of the photos posed and snapped from the ground or from the tops of the locomotives shows anything, anyone Chinese.

Arnold looks over the pages of old photos with a large magnifying glass Dad uses in making his model planes. "The guy on the pole and the guys on the engines could be hiding rifles, do you think?" Arnold asks.

"I don't know," Donald Duk says. "See, there were soldiers to keep us out of the picture. Don't you think we belong in this picture more than any of these white men?"

"I'm white," Arnold Azalea says.

"You're white, but you're not white like these guys. I like you. I don't care what you are."

"I care what you are."

"What am I?"

"Are we fighting? Why?" Arnold asks. "I thought we were on the same side."

"That's what I thought too."

"Mom! Donald Duk's being a snot." Venus shouts through the house and pushes the door to Donald's room open.

"What is going on here?" Penny asks. "Contemporary retrospective existential Yuppie-ismo?"

"Oh, you know, so-so Ionesco! You know," Venus says in a tinny phony upper-crusty British accent.

"Fred Astaire wasn't good at accents either," Penny says. "You sound more like Sartre à la carte."

"Mind your own business, will you! Just shut up! You are not funny!" Donald slams the door to his room closed. Through the door, Donald hears "How Beckett!"

"Tray tray Beckett, madman gazelle."

"Don't make fun of your mother's quest for knowledge," he hears Mom say.

The firecrackers are still exploding all over the streets, in the air, outside. The streets are still crammed with tourists. It's still early. Donald Duk sleeps, dreams, wakes, panics through the books and pictures looking for Chinamen from out of the past, one day in May picks a fight with his only real friend in the whole world for no good reason, and it's still early. He's surprised. It feels much later than it is.

Arnold asks permission to use the phone. Mom and the twins are still up working on their model airplanes. Dad is still at the restaurant. The opera people eat every night in the upstairs banquet room with a balcony looking down Grant.

"I wish to make this call collect," Arnold says into the phone. "Mr. Azalea, please. Tell him it's his son calling." Arnold Azalea waits and sees Donald Duk seeing him. "Hello, Dad? I want to come home now. I no longer feel welcome . . ."

"It was a local call," Donald Duk says irritably. "You could have . . ."

"It's all right, okay," Arnold Azalea says. "It's already done."

The first thing Donald Duk sees as he steps out of his building is the Chinatown Fiddler, already the saddest man in Chinatown, wearing a colored skullcap and trouser bottoms tied to his ankles. The fiddler's monkey is tied to a lampost and watches and screeches at the Fiddler faking and crazing up a kung fu set at the center of a small circle of tourists. Donald Duk passes a Chinatown bar and lounge where the Chinatown Frank Sinatra sings, "I did it my-eeee wayyy," off in a sudden instant of firecracker silence.

Again, this year, the carnival rides—every spoke, every curve, every rise and fall outlined in neon light—are tucked into the dinky Portsmouth Square, in the shadow of Chinatown and Nob Hill in the morning and the tall buildings of the financial district, the TransAmerica Pyramid, the Holiday Inn sawhorse in the afternoon. The lights of the spinning ferris wheel and whirlagigs scrawl candy colors and melted shadows all over the walls of the buildings surrounding the little park. A cement pagoda building with two Chinese restaurants, a Chinese shrine supply store full of Kwan Kungs, Kwan Yins, Choy Suns, Monkey Kings, candles, happy Buddhas, and red shrines in the window, next door to the portrait studio of "the Chinese Richard Avedon," portrait photographer who never heard of Richard Avedon till "the Chinese Marilyn Monroe" of 1966 told him. The Chinese Richard Avedon married the Chinese Marilyn Monroe. Both are getting old now. He's wearing a five-year-old toupee. She's had a neck lift. Round and round the banana yellow, cool lime green, anemic neon red flows over the concrete facade of the proselytizing visionary Buddhist church building across the street, next door to a two-story Chinese restaurant with a glittery tile front.

A tall thin Chinatown kid in a camouflage field jacket, military web belt with an army plastic canteen in a canvas canteen cover, plastic helmet-liner and steel helmet with canvas camouflage cover, blue jeans bloused into the top of highly polished black jump boots laced with white parachute cord carries a Christian Holy Bible with gilt-edged pages and goes from group to crowd— who are waiting for rides or watching ping pong balls bounce off the edges of fishbowls, darts miss balloons, baseballs miss metal milk bottles—before opening his Bible and striking up a conversation.

Donald Duk watches the yellow fake chaplain in his pastel fake war with firecrackers and electronic fake calliope tootles and plips. Donald says, "Don't mess with me," with his shoulders, his chest, his neck, his face, his eyes, and walks on. No one messes with him.

Late. After ten. After midnight. The firecrackers aren't popping now. Empty streets. Night lights in the closed stores. The sad sounds of the Chinatown Fiddler are missing tonight. Gone with the tourists. Arnold will be gone by now too. Another tourist.

Donald Duk walks alone, hands in his pockets, head down, watching his shadow rotate around his feet, listening to his feet. He listens to his feet. Stupid feet. He dreams with his eyes on his stupid feet, one stupid footstep after the other down the alley to the back of Dad's restaurant. Whoops! Strange moves at Dad's back door. Donald Duk slicks into a shadow to watch.

The Crawdad Man passes fifty-pound sacks of rice from inside the restaurant to his son, in the doorway, who passes one sack at a time to the one Frog Twin, who passes the sack to the other Frog Twin, who passes the sack to Dad, who loads it into his van.

"Remember when this truck was red, little sisters?" Dad asks the Frog Twins.

"Remember when Chinese girls of Hollywood used to get

write-ups in the newspaper when they say they're tired, just sick and tired of playing prostitute and exotic bimbos?" one Frog Twin asks.

"I know, I know, you were in *The Good Earth,* girls. I hate that movie. I know you're in the Screen Actors Guild. I hate Oriental actors. So don't talk about acting," Dad says.

"You only say that because you are a heathen."

"I wish Pearl Buck was alive and walk into my restaurant so I can cut out her heart and liver. That's how much I hate that movie."

"Oh, you're right," the other Frog Twin says. "There was that what's-her-name."

"Yeah, her! Whatchamacaller."

"From London, too!"

"But that Bikini was from Malibu."

"I thought she was very pretty."

"Oh, I thought so too. I thought she had a future in the industry."

"She had that great body. One of the first Chinese girls with a body like that."

"Yeah, Body by Fisher."

"But she opened her big mouth."

"Oh, she thought she was . . . was . . ."

"It was Hollywood suicide, what it was."

"Of course, that's what it was. But she thought she was . . . was . . ."

"She was stupid, that's what she was."

"Of course, of course, but she thought she was . . ."

"She thought Hollywood had a conscience."

"Of course . . . Yes, that's it! Conscience."

"It was our chance, though. How many Chinese twins do you see, huh?"

"And that little fella. Whozzit, you know."

"Oh, him. Yeah, I know. Whozzit. He made some news too, didn't he!"

"Well, he was something, the way he carried on."

"Yeah, if all us actors would have rise up and say we're fed up playing prostitute and Suzie Wong . . ."

"Oh, we would change the world!"

"Now, when did Hollywood ever ask you girls to play whores in the movies, huh? Or Suzie Wong?" Dad asks.

"It's the ideal."

"You don't understand the principle involved."

"Just pass the rice, little sisters."

"Ah-Jeh, please! We are old enough to be your mother."

"At least your mother's *younger* sister."

Donald Duk steps out of the shadows and walks up to Dad's van. "Dad," Donald Duk says.

"What's wrong with you? What are you doing out on the street at this time of night? You have to get up early for tai chi."

"Oh, don't scold him, you barbarian! It's New Year, Ah-King! Are you all right, Donald Duk? Hungry?"

"I'm okay. I'm okay. What are *you* doing out at this time of night, Dad?"

"We're going to leave a fifty-pound sack of rice at the door of every apartment on this side of this block."

Uncle Donald Duk steps out of the restaurant with the opera people. "That's all of it, Ah-King!" Uncle Donald Duk turns to the opera people. "I'm an old man. I'm going to ride with Uncle King. I'll meet you around the block. You walk."

"You want to get in the truck?" Dad asks Donald Duk. Donald Duk climbs in and finds himself in the middle, between Uncle Donald Duk and Dad, who's tucking himself in behind the wheel. The Frog Twins ride in the back, sitting on cardboard on the rice sacks.

"Why are you doing this, Dad?"

"Tradition."

"Tradition?" Donald Duk asks. "What tradition?"

Uncle Donald Duk puts an arm around little Donald, smiles

and clears his throat. "It's everybody's birthday, today. The sixth day of the first month of the new year."

"That's right," Dad says.

"And when your father was a boy and was living in Oakland, across the bay, he knew this gambler. Big Jim Chin. He used to leave hundred-pound sacks of rice at every door in Chinatown."

"That's true! Hundred-pound sacks of rice. Your father's such a cheapskate, Donald Duk!" one Frog Twin says.

"Well, fifty pounds is better than nothing, Sis."

"But fifty-pound sacks for just one block! Tsk tsk tsk."

"Not even one block, Sis."

"Just this side of of one block."

"Listen to the movie stars, Uncle Donald," Dad says.

Donald Duk sits up, pulls on Dad's sleeve and leans to whisper into his ear. Dad pulls away and shakes his head. "What! You have something to say? Say it! *Chieee!*"

"I'm afraid to dream," Donald Duk sullens out low.

"Afraid to dream? What does that mean?" Dad asks.

"Everything I dream is true. Or was true. I dreamed we set a world's record, and it's true. I dreamed we laid the last crosstie, and it's true."

"We?"

"The Chinese. The Chinamans who built the railroad. I dream I'm laying track with them when I sleep, and nobody knows what we did. Nobody, just me. And I don't want to be the only one who knows, and it makes me mad to be the only one who knows, and everything I dream makes me mad at white people and hate them. They lie about us all the time."

"No, don't hate all the white people. Just the liars," Dad says.

"We lay the last crosstie yesterday, May 9th. That means to-night I dream the last spike. And I don't want to."

"So?"

"Ah-King! He's a good boy. Aren't you, Donald Duk? Don't yell at him."

"Okay, okay! I yell at *you!* Don't talk! If I bounce the truck with your mouth open, your false teeth will fall out."

"Be nice! Ah-King!" the Frog Twins scold in duet.

"Okay, okay," Dad says and sighs.

"Be cool!"

"Nobody says that anymore!"

"I say that. Cool it. Ah-King, cool it. There! I said it again."

In a softer voice aimed at Donald Duk's ear, Dad says, "When you're ignorant, stupid, don't know nothing, and say Ching Chong Chinaman, that's okay. The stupid are stupid." Dad drives slowly, brakes slowly to a stop and starts slowly around the corner to the left and down the hill to Grant. "Dad, this is a one-way street, and you're going the wrong way. Do you know that?"

In the same softer voice, "But you know truth. The truth came looking for you in the dreams. You go look for the truth in the library. You know what is true. You know what is true," Dad says again. "That makes your life hard, kid. You have the choice. If you say Chinese are ching chong, you have to choose to do it and lie about what you know is true. And you remember one thing too: Soong Gong, the Timely Rain, came to you in your dreams and asked you to go to his hideout and join his heroes. Boys and girls don't dream like that over here. You must be something special. Maybe.

"I read those books all my life. I do the opera," Dad says. "Soong Gong never talked to me. The Marvelous Traveler never came into my dreams to say, 'Soong Gong asks you to join the heroes.'"

Dad drives the loaded van slowly around the block and parks in front of the small front door of an apartment staircase that smells of old old fog-soaked wood and a sweet minty chemical disinfectant.

The opera people form a human chain up the three flights of stairs. Dad, Uncle Donald Duk, the Frog Twins, the Crawdad Man and his son pass sacks of rice out of Dad's van to the chain of opera people. Donald is numb, tired, sleepy, and not making sense to Dad, who always seems to have something to do and always seems to be doing it, with no understanding, no time for those who don't know what to do and aren't doing anything in particular.

Donald Duk climbs the stairs like a zombie, not dead, not alive, up to the third-floor landing and stretches out on a small mountain of rice sacks, when Uncle Donald Duk pokes him in the ribs and hands him a torn and unfolded cardboard box, "Here, kid, sleep on this in case you fart or wet your pants. We don't want to foul the rice. Good boy." Uncle Donald Duk laughs like an idling city bus, with a jolly word to everybody on his way down the stairs.

Donald Duk falls asleep to feet thumping up and down the stairs as Mr. Yin and the five or six opera people move the rice out of the truck up the stairs to pile them up on the landings to three floors. After a breather for Uncle Donald Duk, Dad and the Frog Twins, they pass the sacks of rice down to every room door on the three floors.

Dad lifts Donald Duk off the sacks of rice, the Crawdad Man and Crawdad Jr. pick up the sacks still warm from Donald Duk and pass them to Uncle Donald and the Frog Twins, who drop a sack at each door. Dad carries Donald over his shoulder and leads the way down the stairs to the empty truck. "Everyone! Back to the restaurant for a little midnight snack!" he calls on the way down.

Donald Duk wakes fast, smelling something strange, and is inside the van. Firecrackers blast in the apartment stairway. The Crawdad Man's son jumps into the back of the van laughing. The explosions magnify and sharpen up the stairs and down the hallways. Lights come on in the windows. "I should whack you one," the Crawdad Man says. "Who told you to wake everybody up!"

The opera women boil the water and drop washed rice in for *bok jook*, white jook. They cut and twist the dough for *yow jow gwai*, the doughnuts known as "demons boiled in oil." Dad washes his hands and whips up two huge platters of dry fried *chow fun*.

Donald Duk sits between his dad, King Duk, and Uncle Donald Duk. Uncle Donald Duk drops slices of the *yow jow gwai* on top of his rice porridge. He sinks the slices into the white mush and sprinkles chopped green onions, soy sauce, a few drops of sesame oil, white pepper, boiled peanuts and slices of a thousand-year-old duck egg turned black and purple jelly onto his steaming jook before spooning up and slurping it into his mouth. The restaurant around Donald Duk sounds like babies blowing bubbles in their baths. "Put some *yow jow gwai* in, they're fresh," Dad says. "A real treat."

"Why do you call them *yow jow gwai?*"

"Didn't I hear Uncle Donald Duk tell you that already?"

"Please, please, I'm listening this time. I really want to know. I'm not faking."

"You know the famous tattooed hero Ngawk Fay?"

"Is that the same as Yin the tattooed wrestler?"

"Naw, naw. Different names. Different names in different people. Yin the Wrestler likes tattoos on his body like pictures for the skin. His skin was very pretty too. Oooh, that Lee Shi Shi loved his skin and wanted to touch Yin's skin and his tattoos. Right, Uncle Donald?"

"He remembers Yin the Wrestler. That means he listens some of the time, at least."

"Ngawk Fay is a soldier in old China. To make a long story short, some bad guys make Ngawk Fay look like he desert the army and is a traitor. Ngawk Fay's mother tells him to go to the Emperor and show him his back, and she tattoos words, a slogan on his back, something like *Forever loyal to the Emperor and the nation.* Doesn't work. The Emperor wants to cut off his head. Ngawk Fay hides out and is betrayed by a married couple. They fink on him for the reward. The people give them their own reward. They call the double doughnut *yow jow gwai* and deep fry that couple and cut them up and eat them in jook every day, they hate them so much. And that's the story of *yow jow gwai.*"

Donald Duk watches the flat figure-eights of *yow jow gwai* float on his jook. He misses his late-night TV. The big-screen TV was his new best friend and now he's afraid to watch it, afraid the American Cong will jump him on a newsbrief.

"Dad," Donald Duk says and wants to be asleep, wants Dad to read his mind and make it okay without Donald Duk saying another word. "You know, Dad, the other night, Chinese New Year's Eve," Donald drones slowly then suddenly wants to know, "Dad why don't Chinese people party on their New Year's Eve like everybody else?"

"The old Chinese used to call the last month of the year, 'The monster dies.' It is the worst time for getting into any trouble. You don't want to begin the next year with last year's trouble. So the whole last month, people lie low and get cranky staying out of trouble, and the last night, they stay home to be sure they begin the new year at home with their family, their power, their treasure."

"You especially don't want to get in any fight with anybody. The way you start the year is set the tone for the whole year, and stuff like that," Uncle Donald Duk says.

"Yeah, that was the night I took the P-26A Peashooter up on the roof." Donald Duk turns to Uncle Donald Duk, "You remember."

"Umk," Uncle Donald Duk grunts yes.

"It was 2:30 in the morning. I remember looking at my watch before I took the plane. There was a man on the roof. It's the man they arrested for killing Fisheyes Koo. Homer Lee was sick on the roof when they say Fisheyes was killed."

"Why are you telling me this, now?"

"Dad, do what good nice dads do on TV. Take me to the police."

"And what? Throw you in jail?"

"I saw you on your roof!" one Frog Twin says.

"We were wearing our spring outfits. I remember that little airplane!" the other Frog Twin says.

"And when it caught fire and exploded!" one says. "To think, just up Telegraph Hill Fisheyes is shot at the same time," the other says. "Coincidence," one says. "And it was after the bars close," the other says. "Yes, it had to be around 2:30 because that's when we come out to check the last garbage," one says. "Which they don't put out til 2:15 or 2:20," the other says. "Do you remember seeing us?" one asks.

"Okay, we'll all go to the police. It will serve them right. If they're serious about finding Koo's killer, someone on that Gang Task Force is going to have to wake up and ask you a lot of questions. That's okay with me. But no matter what, you go to your tai chi in the morning."

Dad stands over a heaping platter of *chow fun* and raises his cup. "Happy Birthday to Everybody and the memory of Big Jim Chin." Uncle Donald Duk and the Frog Twins and opera people burst into applause.

Dad rinses the dishes, loads them in a dishwashing basket and runs them through the machine before leaving the restaurant for the Chinatown/North Beach Station.

"How do we know you didn't just see Lee on TV and make all this up?" the police ask. "Tell us something about him you didn't read in the newspaper or hear on TV."

"He's orange. He won't go to the VA."

"What do you mean, he's orange?"

"He says a big fist grabs his heart and squeezes. And his heart hurts and beats too fast, too slow and goes on and off."

"It seems like you can easily check that out with a medical examination, right, Inspector?" Dad says.

"I think you might be right, Mr. Duk," the policeman says. "Tell me, why did you call the media? I thought Chinese didn't like publicity."

"Strategy," Dad says. "The objective is justice for the wrongfully accused Mr. Homer Lee. The strategy is what I call *The Open Society Strategy.*" Dad laughs as the policeman's eyes narrow. "And I own a Chinatown restaurant. What do you mean we're shy about publicity? Every time my restaurant's name appears in Herb Caen's column, my business jumps! Ha ha ha ha . . ."

On the way home from the police station in Dad's van, he asks, "Anybody hungry?"

"No, no, Ah-King!" Uncle Donald Duk says. "Not another midnight snack."

Mom is still awake. Arnold is not in the house. "What happened between you two?" Mom asks. "His family chauffeur came for him in the world's longest car."

17

MAJOR GENERAL G.M. DODGE commands the U.S. Army from the Missouri River to California. The Indian campaigns of 1865 and 1866 shape and move on his orders. He has the chief engineer of the Union Pacific Railroad send a telegram. Donald Duk sees it in his dream: Dated Promontory Utah 10 via Omaha 11 a. Received at Washington May 11th. To Gen. J.D. Cox Secty Interior. The Final connection of Rail was made today at Promontory Summit—one thousand and eighty six (1086) miles from Missouri River and six hundred and ninety (690) miles from Sacramento—It enables the millions of China to find an outlet eastwardly and eventually they will be cultivating the cotton of fields of the South—G.M. Dodge, initialed by Western Union Telegraph clerk, 51 DH Pass.

Donald Duk is sleeping fast. He dreams at the speed of light.

"Up! Up! Up! Rise and run, boys and girls!" Dad! Another early morning. Arnold Azalea's gone. The twins talk about it all the way to sunrise tai chi with Mr. Yin. Donald runs grim and angry. He wonders why nobody sees he's going crazy.

Nobody notices how different he is from everybody else, even from his usual self, even at Uncle's Café on Clay. He feels a little sick, being so isolated in personal weirdness in this crowd of Chinese.

Uncle's Café is a Chinatown coffeeshop peculiar to San Francisco. It's an old-time greasy spoon complete with breaded veal cutlets and hamburgers that squirt grease when you bite into them, flaky pies and a roast prime rib of beef special every day. Here the apple pie may be part of a meal of *wonton* and *chow fun* with roast pork and applesauce, and duck legs and chicken feet during *deem sum* lunchtime, with a strawberry milkshake. Uncle's makes malteds too. The place has an ancient counter covered in some kind of awful plastic hardboard and even more ancient round, swivel-topped soda-fountain stools. And it has wooden booths built during the Great Depression of the thirties, when the largest people were still small and compact and six feet tall was unusually tall. Donald Duk likes the place. He can usually get lost here, studying the art students, the young white actors and cab drivers, who are the only whites and who have kept Uncle's Café, early in the morning, a secret among themselves and make themselves a part of Uncle's atmosphere, crammed hip to hip, knee to knee, elbow to elbow over a tiny table in a booth. The others are older and very old Chinese and with their families. Lots of bacon and eggs and oyster sauce and rice. A few bowls of jook and the long deep-fried doughnuts, *yow jow gwai*, demons boiled in oil. Lots of waffles and pancakes. Uncle's is famous for its crisp Chinatown waffle. Uncle's is famous for its custard pie. Dad and the family have to wait for a booth. They come knowing they will wait. It's part of breakfast at Uncle's Café.

The old bald waiter at Uncle's pops out of the swinging door to the kitchen with plates of food in each hand and more plates stacked up his arms. He throws grabeyes onto people lined up to get in and breathlessly includes them in his constant patter as he lays out hot breakfasts and calls orders into the kitchen. "You hammaneck over ease, sticky potatoes. You by you'self! Sit right dere! Don't afraid! Sit! Yeah! Sit! Beckon anna scramboo, ricee no grave. Oh, Ah-King Sifu! Maestro! How many? Five! Wow! I kick somebody out for you, but bad for business to do things like that. But if you can't wait."

"We can wait, Ah-Bok," Dad says, calling the baldhead Old Uncle. That's a lot of respect.

"Pork chop, poachecks, Frenchie fries, you. Sausage patties, sunnyside ups. Okay. You a waffoo. I get the syrup, don't worry." The bald Chinatown waiter's voice and clatter as he deals his plates of breakfast off his sleeve orchestrates the rise and fall, the ebb and flow of noisy crockery, hoarse patter and the crunch and ding of an old mechanical cash register as customers pass in and out of Uncle's Café.

Mom and Donald Duk cram the little wooden bench on one side of the booth, and the twins pack the other, dressed exactly alike in the *minop* jackets Uncle Donald gave them. Donald Duk can't keep himself from saying, "You know, late at night, on TV, when they have these commercials about terrible diseases and helping the starving and cosmetic surgery. . . ?"

"Oh, I hate those things," Mom says. "I think of all the old rickety folks staying up late to see Don Ameche and Gene Autry again for excape."

"*Esss-cape,* Mom," Venus says low and tries not to move her lips.

"You know what I mean. The traffic is quiet. No banging garbage cans for a while. They should be able to see one old black-and-white movie they saw first run when they were young . . ."

". . . a thousand years ago," Penelope says.

"They didn't have TV a thousand years ago," Mom says. "You little snots, wait till you're old, and everything you like is only on late late at night, and every seven minutes during your *essss-cape* from the miserable right now, a crying starving baby with bulging eyes and bloated belly is stuck in your face!"

"Gee, Mom! You are so emotional!" Venus says.

"You know, you sound very neurotic today," Penny says.

"I was going to say," Donald Duk says to the twins, "you guys in this booth look like mass-produced refugee dolls packed in a green box."

No one laughs. Dad pulls a chair up to the end of the booth and sits. "It's Everybody's Birthday today, so I ordered waffles for everybody."

"Waffles!" Venus whines.

"Daaa-dee!" Penelope whines. "They're fattening."

"Everybody gets their own birthday cake!" Dad grins.

The twins groan. "Baaaad joke," Venus says.

"It's no joke. The waffles here are the filet mignon of waffles."

"Daaa-dee, stop with the food metaphors," Penny says. "They're just too Freudian for our young ears."

"Yeah, Dad, you're worse than Donald Duk and the Cuisinart."

"The waffles as birthday cakes is a nice thought," Mom says. "It shows your father may someday appreciate poetry."

"You could have them make the waffles into a layer cake, Daddy!" Venus says.

"Yeah, with frosting in-between, and all over!" Penny says. "Ask them for chocolate, Daddy!"

The waffles come and the twins slather theirs with butter, strawberry jam, syrup and honey and devour them fast. Mom and Dad watch amazed as they eat their own waffles with butter and artificially flavored maple syrup in smaller bites. Donald Duk nibbles and stares glum glum glum at his waffles. The twins have most of their waffles in their mouths and swallow, making all the noises in their mouths and throats they can, and smack their lips, then daintily wipe their lips and fingers with their napkins dipped in their water glasses.

"I think that's the most disgusting thing I have ever seen," Mom says.

"Not more disgusting than that toy collie getting run over by a Pontiac GTO when we were trying to cross Broadway . . ." Venus says.

"You would have to remember that!"

"You're the one who said *disgusting,* Mom."

"That car's tires were so fat, and that dog was so little!"

"That's exactly what I said just before the Pontiac stopped on it," Penny says.

"Do you remember it crunched?"

"Please, ladies," Mom says, "your mother is eating."

"Pardonay moowah, poor fah-vor, Chef Boy-ar-dee."

"How very continental of you."

Dad finishes his coffee. "You done?" he says to Donald Duk. "I'll drive you to school."

"He's not done with his waffle, Daddy," Venus says.

"Let him finish his birthday cake," Penny says.

"I'm not going to school today," Donald Duk says.

"What do you mean, you're not going to school today?" Mom asks.

"They're nothing but stupid racists there . . ."

"Oh, Donald Duk!" Venus says.

"Hold it, girls, let him talk," Dad says.

"I was just going to ask if there are any old-fashioned, insensitive, machismo, chauvinist pigs there too," Penny says.

"Misogynists, in other words," Venus says.

"Hold it, girls, let him talk," Dad says.

"They're a little snooty maybe," Mom says. "But you know, you can be a snob and not be a racist."

"And vice versa too, Mom," Venus says.

"Or you can be both! Let's be fair, Mom," Penny says.

"That's what I'm trying to say!" Donald says.

"I don't care if they are snooty racists. You're going to school. Do you know how much it costs per day to send you to that school? You're going to school."

"They don't like Chinese . . ."

"Since when did you like Chinese?" Venus asks.

"Tell them they don't like Chinese, not me. I have no problem with Chinese people. You're going to school."

"What's wrong with racists, anyway?" Mom asks. "We have been living with them for over a hundred years now, and we get along with them fine."

"They're supposed to be my friends," Donald Duk says.

"No, they're not," Dad says.

"What about Arnold?" Donald Duk asks.

"What about him?" Dad asks without raising his voice, without missing a beat. "You don't go to school to make friends."

"Ah-King, don't upset him any more than he already is."

"Is he a racist too?" Dad asks.

"No, he's more interested in the Chinese than Donald even," Venus says.

"Who asked you?" Donald snaps.

"I just want to know for my information," Dad says. "The only reason we let him stay in our house and are so nice to him is because he's your friend, not ours. And if he's a racist and not your friend, we should know. And if he is your friend, you should go back to school and back him up. But you're going to school to learn something, no matter what."

Mr. Meanwright's classroom is dark for the slide show illustrating his lecture. The old photos out of his dreams, out of the library books, warm up the screen hanging over the chalkboard.

"Unlike other immigrant groups, the Chinese came to America with no intention of staying, settling or pioneering. They were called *sojourners.*" Mr. Meanwright drones and buzzes in the dark. Donald Duk hears this from all his teachers and is surprised he's flashing hot blood and angry now at what he hears all the time.

That picture of the Chinese tearing out the crosstie that replaced theirs is bright light and dark shadow on the wall. "These Chinese who worked on the Central Pacific were called *Crocker's Pets.*" There is a face that might be Donald Duk's. Donald Duk sees and looks harder as Mr. Meanwright recites on, "Their passive philosophy and noncompetitive nature rendered them ripe for exploitation and victimization. As the historian McLoed says, the

Chinese failed in the gold fields and were driven by poverty and
timidity to help build the Central Pacific leg of the transcontinental railroad." He changes the slide. The photo of the meeting of the
engines at Promontory appears.

"Excuse me, Mr. Meanwright. You are incorrect, sir," Donald
Duk says louder than he expects.

"Lights, please," Mr. Meanwright says. "Let us see who belongs
to this voice out of the dark."

"Mr. Meanwright, what you just said about the Chinese is not
true."

"And you are offended, Mr. Duk. How many of you saw Mr.
Duk on the news this morning? Freeing an innocent, though what
some might regard as an unsavory man is a very noble act, Mr.
Duk." Mr. Meanwright leads the class in applause. Arnold cheers.
"Now what offends you, Mr. Duk?"

"Yessir, I am offended," Donald Duk says in an agreeable way.
A nervous buzz and hush dries the air and shrinks the wet people
dry.

"Well, I never said I was perfect, did I, Mr. Duk. Please, en-
lighten me."

"You are . . . sir, Mr. Meanwright, not correct about us being
passive, noncompetitive. We did the blasting through Summit
Tunnel. We worked through two hard winters in the high Sierras.
We went on strike for back pay and Chinese foremen for Chinese
gangs, and won. We set the world's record for miles of track laid in
one day. We set our last crosstie at Promontory. And it is badly
informed people like you who keep us out of that picture there."
Donald Duk jerks his chin up to look down his face with killer eyes
at the slide of the Last Spike ceremony, still easy to see, like a faded
painting projected on the wall. Everyone in the room avoids Donald Duk's eyes but follows his gesture to the screen. The slide
changes back to an old grainy shot of the Chinese in the Sierra
Nevadas, in the first year, working above the snowline. The white
foreman standing to the side of work on the right of way is lost

behind his beard, fur hat and puffy bearskin coat. The Chinese with picks and shovels in their hands work in *minop* jackets, like everyone in class has on. Everyone in class looks straight into the eyes of a young Chinese boy in the midground, turning toward the camera and smiling. His hat is pushed back off above his forehead. The face is Donald Duk's. No one asks to snap off the lights to see the face clearly.

"I have the books right here," Arnold Azalea says, pulling books out of his briefcase and piling them on his desk.

"We didn't do all of that being passive and noncompetitive, sir."

"The world's tracklaying record was set . . ." Mr. Meanwright ponders

"April 29, 1869," Donald Duk says. "A Thursday, as I remember."

"As you remember, Mr. Duk?" the teacher says.

"Chinese set the record—1200 of us—and the history books don't have one of our names down. But the eight Irishmen who lifted rail off the flatcars with us, their names are the only names. . ."

"That's right. Mr. Duk is correct, Mr. Meanwright. We checked the books out of the library, and here they are."

"Gentlemen, boys, you have caught me completely unprepared for . . ." The lights go out. There's big thump on the door and it flies out of its casing and falls flat inside the classroom. Kwan Kung, red-faced, black-bearded, hairy arching eyebrows, green and blazing gold robe and armor, stands on one leg in the doorway. He brings his leg down and strikes another pose.

"Ha ha ha! I smell a room full of paaaaassivity! Arrrggghhh!" Kwan Kung says. Drums and gongs beat and crash in the hallway. Characters out of Cantonese opera are kicking down classroom doors all over the school. Kwan Kung charges around the room lit by the light streaming through the door and the slats of the Venetian blinds. Up and down the aisles between the desks he brandishes his Black Dragon Doh, never acknowledging, never touching any of the students so close they can touch him. He returns to the doorway and strikes another pose and with a grand gesture grabs the tips of the long pheasant feathers arching out of his helmet.

Out in the hall a voice—Dad's voice?—booms behind Kwan Kung. "This free demonstration of the fine art of Cantonese opera courtesy of Duk Lau Opera. Now appearing at the Sun Sing Theater in the heart of Chinatown."

Kwan Kung twirls his weapon and strikes another pose. A kid from the opera company runs in and holds his hand out to Mr. Meanwright. "Here are the hinge pins to your door," the kid says, drops the steel pins clinking into Mr. Meanwright's hand, and leaves.

"Happy New Year!" the voice in the hall calls, and a pack of firecrackers snickering a burning fuse drops at the doorway of every room. Everyone in the class yells and dives for cover. Mr. Meanwright stands with his eyes on replay. Donald Duk grins at him. *"Goong hay fot choy,"* Donald Duk says.

18

Arnold Azalea's parents sit at the Duk's dining room table. It is cleared of model-making now. Donald Duk and Arnold Azalea stand together, looking serious and contrite. A statuette of Kwan Kung on his horse, Red Rabbit, stands on the bookshelf behind them. Mom releases the handles of a small two-piston espresso machine. "The secret of nice foamy steamed milk for the cappuccino is to start with the spout at the bottom and work your way to the top slowly."

"That's how we make love, not cappuccino," Dad says.

"Don't I wish!" Mom squeals.

Arnold Azalea's dad looks up at the model planes hanging from the ceiling. They glow incandescent above his head in this dim shadowy room before the lights are snapped on. "Ah, these are the model airplanes Arnold was talking about," he says. "Which of these did he build?"

"He was working on a model of the P-38 Lightning," Dad says.

"Don't worry, Arnold. I will finish your P-38 for you," Mom says.

"And I'll pack it with firecrackers and cherry bombs. Like that Fokker triplane."

"The Fokker triplane!" Arnold's dad enthuses like a kid. Dad's Fokker triplane is not painted in airplane dope. Each wing is covered with different-colored tissue paper. A face is watercolored on the bottom of the plane. Open hands are painted on the undersides and topsides of each wingtip. "It certainly isn't the Red Baron's triplane," Arnold's dad says and moves closer. "Who is this, if I might ask."

"That is Yin the tattooed wrestler. He is one of the 108 heroes of an old book I read as a kid, that's all."

"Do the three wings have any meaning for the tattooed wrestler?"

"He was the 108 outlaws' official poet and calligrapher. He is their best musician too. Triple threat. And he is the tattooed wrestler, good with the staff, like that fella Little John in Robin Hood. Only Yin is better-looking, very handsome."

"Fascinating," Arnold's dad says. "Oh, yes, the GeeBee Racer!" He bends over backward and looks under the stub-winged, stub-tailed GeeBee Racer with its cute wheelpants. It's a cartoonist's plane. It looks like R. Crumb zapped back to the thirties to design this plane. "Do you think the aircraft of today have lost something in their design, King? The little GeeBee Racer was a cute whimsical little flier, wasn't she?"

"Yeah, for whimsy, I like the GeeBee Racer the best," Dad says.

"Would I use the word *whimsy* to describe the GeeBee?" Mom asks herself out loud, like Greta Garbo. But the twins aren't here to respond, and Donald Duk can't, because the less he says the better right now.

"Why do you pack these wonderful planes with fireworks?" Arnold's dad asks.

Dad serves Arnold's mom a cappuccino as he speaks, "So they will explode and blow up when I set them afire and fly them," and goes on to serve a cappuccino to Arnold's dad.

"Burn them?" Arnold's dad says.

"That's what I keep saying," Mom says. "Burn them? That's crazy, huh! See, I'm telling you, Ah-King, it's crazy."

"I believe Arnold would like to keep his. In fact, I'm sure he would like to finish building it, and we would like to keep it."

"Why, Mrs. Azalea?" Dad asks.

"Why? It will be something he made with his own two hands. Why burn it up and explode it after all the work he put into it?"

"Not to mention the fire hazard you have with all these bombs and firecrackers in the house!" Mom says.

"That's why I put in the sprinkler system two years ago. It's the greatest," Dad says.

"The greatest, he says."

"I really don't see why anyone would want to burn these little airplanes. They're works of art!" Arnold's mom says.

"You used to burn yours, right?" Dad asks Arnold's dad.

"Yes, I did . . ."

"You used to make model airplanes?" Arnold's mom asks her husband.

"As a boy, yes. And what man still has the model planes he made as a boy?" Arnold's dad asks.

"You didn't tell me."

"I was twenty-five when I met you. I hadn't thought of a model plane in ten or twelve years already."

"And you burned them?"

Dad bursts out laughing like a drunken pirate in an old Errol Flynn movie. "Ha ha ha ha ha ha!"

"Ah-King ah! Be polite!" Mom scolds.

"He burned them, Daisy. Didn't I say he burned them?"

"I had to see if they flew. That was first. And flying, well, they get banged-up beyond restoration to their original splendor after a few flights. How do you do away with a model you have spent days, perhaps weeks building and finishing? It is an airplane. A little airplane, like you say, babe, but it is a real airplane that flies. You can't bury the thing. It's not dead. And you can't lose it or abandon it like an unwanted pet. It is too fragile not to destroy. To see it burn up in midair or explode in flight—that is how an airplane should die. In flight. In its medium, so to speak."

"I can tell you read a lot," Mom says. "That was so flowing, so Robert Lowell and Norman Rockwell! And it sounds like a delicious pagan ceremony to me. Fun for savages, but after all the time we have spent putting together 108 of these things—two wings, three wings, one wing, ay-ya-yay . . . Then to just blow them up."

"Life is war, Mommy," Dad charms out of his smile. "You want to keep your know-how and build more know-how with it, not get hung up admiring what you made and get all sentimental about it, little airplanes or . . ." Dad says and turns toward Donald Duk and Arnold Azalea as his smile shrinks, the hawkeyes brighten and aim, ". . . a big railroad. Which brings me to you two. You!" He nods at Donald Duk. "If you're mad at the white history books and the teacher's telling lies about the Chinese in your face, good!"

"Ah-King! You sound Attila the Hun!"

"I am Attila the Hun, Mommy, " Dad sings without taking his eyes off Donald Duk. "If I get mad at Arnold Azalea because of books he didn't write, no good." Donald Duk lowers his head. "He is your friend," Dad continues. "All he knows about Chinese, as far as you know, is you. You say, he wants to know the truth. You say, you and Arnold dream the same dreams about trains at night. You should have the brains to reckon it out: in this war he is your ally. Do you think people are going to like him more for backing you up in class today? If you want to be stupid and call him a white racist and that kind of stuff, that's your business."

"I don't," Donald Duk says.

"Lift up your head, young man. Who are you talking to?"

Donald Duk lifts his head a little. "You . . ."

"Who?"

"You, Dad."

"Then look at me," Dad says. "Now what were you saying?"

"I don't . . ."

"You don't what."

"I don't want to be stupid and call Arnold Azalea a white racist and stuff like that."

"Then tell him you're sorry and shake hands."

"We did already," Donald Duk says.

"Yessir," Arnold Azalea says. "We did already."

"Not in front of me."

Donald Duk holds his hand out to Arnold Azalea. "I'm sorry, Arnold. I was wrong."

They shake hands and turn to Dad. "Thank him," Dad says.

"Thank you, Donald."

"No, Donald, you thank Arnold!" Dad says.

"Thank you, Arnold."

"You're welcome." They shake hands again.

"You boys still friends?"

"Yessir," Arnold Azalea says.

"Of course," Donald Duk says.

"I now pronounce you man and wife," Mom says. "Okay, okay, enough of these pagan ceremonies for one day. Donald make yourself and Arnold a hot chocolate with the espresso machine. Or would you prefer a cappuccino, Arnold?"

"I'm eleven years old, Mrs. Duk."

When will you start calling me Auntie Daisy, the way I ask you? I have been drinking coffee since I was four, and it hasn't stunted my growth. But it's up to you."

"May I try a cappuccino, Dad?" Arnold Azalea asks. "Mom?" he asks, leaning forward a little.

"You say at twelve years of age a Chinese child is no longer a child, King?"

"The party's over." Dad says, "No more coddling and pampering. No more doting . . ."

"Awww, that's terrible!" Arnold Azalea's dad says. "Well, son, as a farewell to your childhood . . . sure, enjoy your first cappuccino."

"Good, I'll make it," Donald Duk says.

"Then I . . ." Arnold fumbles softly, then clears his throat and speaks up, "then we don't have to go home right away, do we?"

"No, son. King and I have talked it over, and I'm afraid you can stay for the rest of Chinese New Year. Ummm-hmm. This actually seems to be the only place for all of us to be, right now."

"In our house?" Mom asks slow and sweet.

"Ha ha ha. San Francisco at Chinese New Year, I meant to say. But for Arnold, yes, right now, I think this house is the place for him."

Donald and Arnold in their pajamas, in their beds, in the dark, talk low across Donald Duk's room. Now and then a firecracker snaps outside. Now and then a pack of firecrackers rattles and piles cracking crackers. "You made your folks come all the way back from Hawaii just to see us shake hands?"

"Wasn't it great?"

"Yeah."

"Are you still scared of what you're going to dream?"

"No."

"That's great."

"Yeah."

"I bet we're the first kids to make Mr. Meanwright read books, huh?"

"Can you believe it? He never even heard of Kwan Kung before."

"The god of war, plunder, literature . . ."

"Yeah, the god of fighters, blighters and writers."

"Wow, what a great day it's been, huh, Donald?"

"Yeah." The streets outside are empty. No parked cars. No foot traffic. The gutters are full of the paper bodies of exploded firecrackers. The streetsweeping machine will wet the paper down . . . mush it up with its twirling stiff-bristled brooms, spread the mush around and sweep a little of it away. What's left will dry into a tough papier-mâché in the gutters. Everywhere more blown firecracker bodies. More cardboard congealing in the streets. Weeks after Chinese New Year bits of the papier-mâché skin will still cling to the street and the sides of the curbs. Donald Duk hears the Chinatown Fiddler out on the street again, with his monkey and his tin cup, playing sad sad sounds wailing off the walls and still glass. Donald Duk hears Chinatown's old Chinese Ricky Nelson wail and screech slow and Chinese out of some club, "Where's this place caaawalled . . . Low-own-leeee Stree-eee-eee?" to the sad double-string in the street. American Cong! No, it's Lee Kuey! Both are Lees. Donald Duk is a Lee. Coincidence. A dream. Don't ask. All the Black Tornado's muscles balloon and pull at their roots pounding rage. It's the battle-axe freak who likes to run naked into one end of a battle and come out the other covered in layers of drying blood, with a bloody axe in each hand. He turns into the Chinatown alley and stalks on down toward Donald Duk, who feels smaller and smaller. The Black Tornado still has his clothes on. That's a good sign, Donald Duk thinks. He does not want this to become the dream he hates the most: trapped in a huge empty building, being chased for no reason at all. It's that dark. The alley seems that endless. Lee Kuey's axes are still slung on his belt. That's a good sign. Lee Kuey's face is all bulging muscles, a bad case of biceps possesses his head. He stops, still several steps away. Donald can see Lee Kuey from head to toe without moving his eyes. "My master, Soong Gong, the darling Timely Rain, who sees good in me where no one else does, instructs me to tell you the Black Tornado is also the only one of the 108 heroes nicknamed *Stupid Ox* and *The Monster*. I am the lowest of the low. The flame of my virtue and natural nobility is more dim than my hatred and anger, but not completely out. Ha ha ha. Remember me, boy. I am the only one to eat the flesh of his dead mother, because I was hungry and knew she loved me, and still be counted one of the stars of earthly fiends. I am the only one to murder a little boy and still be counted a hero. Because I did it out of stupid loyalty and his father was our enemy, everything sort of worked out. Don't back away from me, boy. I thought you and me were alike, kid. Anger! Hate! I thrive on it. The joy of the stupid. But I see you're only angry. And you're a little better than me. You better be. Because I am the lowest of the low. Don't you dare try to be lower than me. For I'm bound to protect my position, if you understand. Here!" he says and pulls a red envelope out of his bag. *"Goong hay fot choy!"*

Epilog

The Fifteenth Day
Arnold Azalea's parents come to the restaurant at three for an early supper with Arnold, Donald, the twins and Daisy Duk. The boys and the twins have to meet at the White Crane Club to stretch the dragon at five. Mom seats the Azaleas and the family at a large round table at the back of the crowded restaurant. "We're eating nothing special tonight," she says, nodding to the waiter to start serving. "Crawfish appetizer, in honor of our missing friends, the Crawdad Man and his son. Fish maw soup—its taste loses nothing in translation, like its name. A beef brisket and turnip casserole. Steamed catfish with black bean sauce. Some nice pea vines that are in season for the next two weeks. A steamed chicken with oil and green onions. Rice, of course, and almond pudding for dessert. That should hold us till after the parade and opera."

"Sounds marvelous," Arnold's mom says.

"Oh, it's very ordinary home cooking kind of things. It's a nice change after all these rich banquets," Mom says.

"Where is King," Arnold dad asks, "in the kitchen, preparing our dinner?"

"Oh, Ah-King will not be joining us for dinner. He went into seclusion and, carnivore that he is, went vegetarian as part of preparing for his role in the opera tonight. We'll see him in the opera, after the parade. These things go on forever, so don't worry about missing anything. To tell you the truth, I really don't understand them that much. I like watching the audience. You'll see. I don't want to spoil it for you," Mom says and takes a breath. The Crawdad Man and Crawdad Jr. stand by the round banquet table with funny smiles on their faces. "Oh, just in time! Or should I say, it's about time, you two! Please, sit!" Mom says. "We're all family here. Don't be so formal and make me get up and sit down again." The Crawdad Man and Crawdad Jr. sit.

"This is the Fifteenth Day. They say this is the night for lovers to meet and take long walks because, traditionally, tonight is the night people show their fancy lanterns, and the light they cast is soft and warm and conducive to romance."

"Are you taking acting classes again, Mom?" Venus asks.

"No, that's her Katherine Hepburn impression," Penny says.

"You know, there is a famous fairy tale about the Fifteenth Day and lanterns and love," says the Crawdad Man. "The Fifteenth Day is the last day of the New Year celebration. People show their lanterns like Americans decorate their houses with Christmas lights. The lanterns get pretty fancy—birds with wings that move, big dragon boats with people that move around the deck. In this one county seat, there is a greedy, cheating, corrupt prince. At the last minute he wants 365 lanterns for his estate. He sends his goons out to get the lantern maker, then locks him up in a room with a candle and gives him a day and a half to make them. How can he do that? Impossible. Hopeless. He works and doesn't sleep and makes only eighty-one lanterns, but out of the candle flame grows a beautiful woman made of fire. The Candlewick Fairy. And she waves her hand and, ooh, beautiful lanterns appear lit all over the estate—284 lanterns in all. With the eighty-one lanterns the lantern maker made, there are the 365 the bad prince wants. She tells the lantern maker never to tell how these lanterns appeared and returns to the candlewick.

"The prince is amazed. He tortures the lantern maker to find out how he made the lanterns. The lantern maker doesn't speak, even under more torture, when the Candlewick Fairy suddenly appears. The prince falls in love with her on the spot and chases her. She runs from lantern to lantern and finally burns the place down. The lantern maker marries the Candlewick Fairy, and they open a lantern-and-candle shop and live happily ever after."

"Is that a real story, Mommy?" Venus asks.

"I can't say I ever heard it before, but it is a nice story. Thank Uncle Crawdad Man, girls."

"Thank you, Uncle," the twins say.

"Does it really matter if it's real? If it's a nice story, that's all that matters," Arnold's mom says.

"It's the real Chinese story, like 'Goldilocks and the Three Bears.' Everybody knows it. Ah-Daisy, you're born here, your folks are Christians. You don't hear the Chinese stories like Chinese children. That's why you don't understand more of the opera."

"You sound just like my pagan husband, the way you all persecute Christians," Mom says. "See what I have to put up with?" She stands and wipes her mouth, drops the napkin on her chair too daintily and out of a plastic shopping bag pulls white sweatshirts with the emblem of the White Crane Club printed on them. She passes sweatshirts to the twins, Arnold Azalea, Crawdad Jr. and Donald Duk. "Put these on and get down to the White Crane Club. You're running inside the dragon in tonight's parade. We will meet you inside the opera, afterwards. Got all that?"

"I'm going to run inside the dragon. All my dreams of puberty have come true in my adolescence," Venus Duk says.

"You're so lucky, Donald. You're still in puberty," Penny Duk says.

"Would you say this story you told about the woman who grows out of the candle flame is known outside of China?" Arnold's dad asks.

"If you would say 'Little Red Riding Hood' is known outside of California."

"You are thinking of something, I can tell," Mom says. "Was this story done as opera, ever?"

"Oh, yes. A very beautiful opera—*The Candlewick Fairy,*" the Crawdad Man says.

"*The Candlewick Fairy* could be done as an opera, set in Saigon and the Tet Offensive."

"Or the other way around. Everyone knows this story and knows New Year is a bad time for the capital cities to show off bright lights, especially if you're at war."

"Why do you say war? There is no war in *The Candlewick Fairy,* is there?"

"No, those are other stories."

"Oh, other stories about capitals burned down on New Year?"

"On the Fifteenth Day."

"The Fifteenth Day? Other stories with burning capitals on the same day as the fairy tale?"

"Yes."

"That's the story. Everyone who grew up with the fairy tale and the stories expected the Tet Offensive, one New Year or another. Then when Saigon makes a display of burning lights to show its security and prosperity . . . It's *The Candlewick Fairy.*"

"The war is over, Crawdad Man."

"Just think," Arnold's dad says, "if the people in the War College and the Joint Chiefs and the generals had read a fairy tale, they might not have blundered with such humiliating consistency. I'm not saying we might actually have won the war. Too many conditions had to change to put us in a position to win. But had we considered the fairy tale in our intelligence and strategy, we might have been able to lose a little less unmistakably."

"My husband is a frustrated artist. He knows what he wants to say, but he doesn't know what art to use to say it best," Arnold's mom says.

"So, I'm a crass successful businessman with dreams."

"Why do we millionaires believe one has to be poor to produce great art?" Mom asks. Arnold's mom and dad laugh. The twins fake laugh, and open and close their mouths like puppets.

"Mother is the necessity of invention," Venus says.

"I *beg* your pardon," Mom raises her eyebrows.

"See, the rich already produce everything people really *need,* Mom. There's nothing left for the poor to make but art." Penelope Duk bats her eyes, muscles up her cheeks and squeaks, "Boop boopy doo."

"Oh, it's Bette Midler doing Lily Tomlin getting revenge on Shirley Temple," Donald Duk says.

"Now, don't disparage Shirley Temple. She was the Candlewick Fairy of my progressive all-American childhood. There, Crawdad Man! Ha ha ha."

Mr. Yin is not here to stretch the dragon. He is at the Sun Sing, playing in the opera band. The White Crane Club's Sifu is a short man barely taller than Donald Duk. He is a thin wiry man with layers of muscle all over his body like a croissant. On his arms, up his neck, the muscles fold and slither over each other like colored boa constrictors. He leads the dragon runners in white sweatshirts and black pants in a run down the hill through Chinatown to a recently finished steel-and-concrete building on the edge of the financial district. Nothing in the building is finished. No signs. No paint.

The dragon stretches in "S" loops from one wall to the other across the fresh cement floor of the corner storefront. The place smells like cement.

The Sifu will carry the head. He chooses Donald Duk to run directly behind him, carrying the neck. Behind Donald Duk, the Sifu lines up progressively taller kids for a section, then down to short kids for the center sections then up again to tall kids carrying the tail. They pick the dragon up by climbing inside the open belly and lifting poles. They carry the dragon out of the smell of cement and dusty dark of the unfinished storefront and stretch the dragon's scaly snake's body. The fins and eagle claws are painted on paper and hang from the silk stretched over the bamboo skeleton. A row of electric light bulbs is strung along the top of the tunnel inside the dragon. It's like being inside one of Dad's airplanes. The ordinary extension cords carrying juice for the lights are taped together into a rope and plugged into a cable from the generator on the back of the flatbed truck carrying the dragon's drums, cymbals and gongs, already beating. And the five dancing lions run the lights of their eyes on hidden flashlight batteries. Donald can see through the dragon's skin.

The light bulbs dim up and go as bright as they go. The lights inside catch in the silk dragonskin and it's not as easy for Donald Duk to see where he's going. Blind in the dragon's belly, he has to watch the Sifu's feet in front of him. He has to keep a certain distance to keep the bit of dragon neck between them from sagging.

Donald Duk translates the Sifu's instructions for Arnold Azalea. The twins are tall and farther down the tunnel. "When you get tired just yell," Donald translates, "and somebody from the outside will trade places, understand? Keep your eye on who's running in front of you, and stop when he stops or you'll bump him, knock him down and the dragon will collapse, which will be a disaster."

This is the third day Dad is alone in a small room at the back of the theater. He cooks for himself, eats alone, looks no one in the face, acknowledges no one around him, does not speak and seems not to hear, as he goes clean into the role. No TV. No radio. No records. No tapes. No magic.

Before putting on his makeup, Dad goes to the kitchen to pay his respects at the shrine to Wah Gong Sifu, set up on a wooden table covered with contact paper. The glassed portrait of the god of opera people is propped up against a two-pound coffee can. An empty tuna fish can painted red and filled with sand serves as an incense burner. A bottle of Johnny Walker Red filled with tea, a plain steamed chicken on a platter, a hunk of roast pig on a platter, three little bowls of rice, three little teacups, three sets of chopsticks and a pile of ceremonial fake paper money and fake gold and silver ingots printed on paper are arranged in front of the incense burner. Every actor and musician and stagehand comes to pay their respects before the performance. Each fusses a little with the teacups or the rice bowls and chopsticks before they strike a match and set fire to a handful of fake money and drop it, one burning bill at a time, into a brass bowl at the foot of the table. They clasp their hands and bow three times, light incense and bow three times, poke the sticks of smoldering incense into the sand and pour fake Johnny Walker Red on the floor. Only the actor who plays Kwan Kung burns real money and serves the opera house real Kentucky bourbon.

No one passing him in the narrow backstage hallway as they pass the dressing rooms to the toilet and kitchen says a word or looks him in the face. They already treat him as if he is Kwan Kung, as if his eyes will kill. He keeps his eyes down. He is alone in his dressing room, surrounded by the pieces of his costume and the pads and braces he must put on first. He begins his makeup. The red is on—the eyes. He will put the beard on after he gets himself into his complex costume. He is ready to powder the greasepaint and feels another body breathing in his dressing room and stops, casts his eyes down and rages inside iron skin.

"Excuse me, Maestro! I'm sorry to disturb you. I just want to thank you. Your son is a perfect host. He even asked me if I had eaten yet. Bye." And Dad feels the body leave and himself breathing alone in his dressing room.

He looks into his mirror and sees Kwan Kung. "It's been a long time," Dad says.

"When the guy in front of you lifts his pole, you lift yours. When he puts his down, you put yours down," Donald Duk translates by feel and guesswork and by what the twins told him before.

The dragon is the end of the parade, the last to start. The two trucks of the five lions start rolling slow and the bands on the back beat hard on the big drums and whang the throaty wail and shimmering teeth out of the gongs and cymbals. The five lions that lead the dragon mount the legs of their two boys and languidly begin dancing after their flatbed trucks. They stretch their necks, dart looks this way and that, shake their beards, flap their mouths, charge and withdraw, leading the close of the parade down Market Street.

The Sifu takes the glowing head of the dragon. The lights inside catch in the stretched silk skin and dragon's flesh seems to be light. The entire dragon is a lantern. The head of a camel. Horns of a deer. Beard and mane of a lion. Body of a snake. Legs of a tiger. Claws of an eagle. Fins and tail of a fish. Where the crowd has already thinned, Donald Duk glimpses the whole dragon reflected in the dark of a closed department store window.

And the dragon is a lantern, he sees. The dragon does seem to fly, swimming and snaking in the low sky over the street. Up ahead, kids in robes and papier-mâché masks of the Eight Immortals walk along in the parade, waving fans and carrying lanterns, representing an old Chinese language school Donald Duk never attends, though his enrollment is paid up. The dragon now and then accelerates and turns, beginning a twist in the body across the width of the street. The body runs by the crowd with the flop and squeak of rubber-soled shoes and a blur of light that makes the people oooh and scares some children to crying. The tromp of all the feet inside the dragon and the beating and banging band crashing crazy time gong gong on and on run twang run run run. Donald huffs and puffs and can't get a real breath. He wants out. "Out!" he cries, and a body jumps in. A girl! And he's out in the air, suddenly still in the cool. He grabs a towel and trots after the dragon. It can't be the girl from the *deem sum* people's camp in the dream. It can't be.

All the great marching drill teams are marching tonight. Drill teams dressed as *vaqueros*. Drill teams in tuxedos and top hats twirling pink rifles. Drill teams in three-piece suits doing precision manual of arms with attaché cases and umbrellas. Year after year Donald Duk sees it all. But this is the first time he's run in the dragon. He's running on railroad tracks. Cable car tracks? Streetcar tracks? He can't take the time to find out which while he's looking for the girl from the *deem sum* camp, and he slips on the shine of a track and falls. The dragon's neck comes down, and there's an arm under his arm, hauling him to his feet, and another hand shoving the pole back into his hands. He doesn't think to see whose hands save him and runs on without a mind. His legs run on automatic pilot.

He walks fast, intent on keeping up with the dragon and seeing if the girl is the girl from the dreams. He's glad the dreams are gone. He believes the dreams are gone. The last spike—the photos snapped slowly on glass plates—seems the end of the story. Donald Duk looks into the crowd for faces he knows. The white sweatshirts and black pants make sense now. White to reflect the light inside the dimly lit dragon. Black to be invisible and give the dragon flight. The thumping running shoes, the thumping hearts roll a pattering fleshy thunder tuned to the dragon's drums and tooth-chattering brass. The faces of all the people he ever pleased, the gang kids who laugh at him in nightmares he doesn't have anymore. He's not looking for the faces of the people he wants to see him. He watches the faces change as they catch sight of the dragon. Faces he's never seen before and will never see again. No parents. No Frog Twins. No Mr. Meanwright. Nobody from the public library, the school, no Chinatown Fred Astaire. Inside the dragon, he can't see the faces in the crowd through the glare of the dragon's light in its skin. Up Powell, down Sutter, up Stockton, down California, up Kearney, he seems running forever.

The parade is endless. It runs with him, into the opera, where the rhythms, gongs and cymbals crash and twang the same as the dragon. The lights are on inside the opera house. They never dim.

Everyone is running inside the dragon, where the lights are on.
The sharp little woodpecker-rhythms of the tone boxes and ma-
rimba bars and bells get in the depressions by the temples and sinus
cavities of everyone's skulls and echo like cherry bombs going off
in the girls' lavatory at school. Children sit on the stairs leading up
to the stage and fall asleep while the band crashes cars and planes.
On the auditorium floor, a father walks up and down the raked
aisle, rocking and patting his baby, while onstage a woman in
white and red makeup and fancy hair sings the sound of mating
electrical charges.

The Chinatown Fiddler is in the opera band, playing his double-string fiddle. A vaguely familiar man from where Donald Duk
can't remember plays a huge version of the double-string fiddle.
The body of the big fiddle looks like a short conga drum. The
sounding board where the fiddle's bridge sits is a snakeskin drum
head. It cries and sullenly threatens like Joan Crawford in the late-
night movies. The Frog Twins sit in the audience with shopping
bags full of snacks, their knitting and their folding fans. Donald
Duk hears gossip all around him. Arnold Azalea's dad asks,
"When are they going to quiet down so they can listen?" And
Mom laughs and offers him coconut candy. "Go on and talk as
loud as you want," Mom says. "That's the fun. Everyone does it."
She smiles. "I understand the audience better than the opera anyway."

"This isn't quite what we expected when you said opera."

"Well, it is loud!" Mom says. The cast banquet after the opera is
loud. *Chi mooey,* the finger-counting game Dad plays with Uncle
Donald Duk, is loud. "Three!" Dad calls, throwing three fingers
while Uncle Donald throws no fingers, a fist. All the fingers showing add up to three. Dad wins a round and Uncle Donald, the
loser, has to drink a shot of Scotch and chant on numbers, fingers,
winning, losing in the same rhythm as the opera, as the dragon, as
the lions, as the loud engines of the boat to Angel Island.

"Say, what kind of birds fly at night?" Dad asks. A silly question

that hushes everyone and sets them listening to the dark around
them. "Are there coyotes on Angel Island? Didn't I read about
wild goats? Deer?" Without a discouraging word, Dad makes everyone stop confessing their ignorance, stop apologizing for sounding stupid, and all their oohs and ahhs remembering just what
they've seen tonight. The food. The opera. The parade. The
dragon. Dad's silly question has them listening to the silence.
Nothing. Not a car. Not a siren. No distant train whistle in the
night. No fight in the alley. No car stereo booming at the curb.
"Do hawks fly at night? Police dogs set loose at the end of World
War II by the MPs went wild and bred in the hills behind Pearl
Harbor and Waikiki and threatened Honolulu at night when they
came out to forage in packs. Did you read about that?" Not a
whimper. Not a breath. Not a howl.

They unpack the planes from the cardboard boxes they've carried over. Down on the dock by the old Immigration Detention
Station, they light the fuses to the planes as Dad tells them the
Thirty-Six Stars of Heavenly Spirits, the Seventy-Two Stars of
Earthly Fiends. Donald Duk holds the P-26A he made, starts the
little engine and lights the fuse. He sees Dad has painted the face
of Walt Disney's Donald Duck on the underside of the cowl and
the arms and chest of Lee Kuey, the Black Tornado, on the wings
and belly.

Several planes are flying already. They are only sounds in the
dark, occasionally a silhouette against the lights of San Francisco.
Silently they, one by one, poof into flame and glow like lanterns as
the Frog Twins, Mom and the twins, Arnold Azalea and his parents, the Crawdad Man and Crawdad Jr., Uncle Donald Duk and
Donald Duk launch the last planes. Briefly, all 108 arc in flight and
aglow before they start exploding in midair, and Donald Duk remembers dreams, the 108 horsemen galloping across the cloud
over the ten miles of track just laid by the 1,200 Chinese and eight
Irishmen. And very quickly they are all gone. The light, the faded
explosions over the dark bay. Not a sound. Not a flash. All 108

stick-and-paper model airplanes gone. "Anybody hungry?" Dad asks. The flight of years of nights of work around the dining room table covered with an inch-thick sheet of plywood, launched, flown, burned out of the low-slung sky over the bay in maybe five minutes. Less than ten minutes . . . like everything else, it begins and ends with *Kingdoms rise and fall, Nations come and go,* and food.

COLOPHON

This book was set in Adobe Garamond type and smyth sewn for readability and durability.